Essence

Harrie Williams

Copyright © 2023 Harrie Williams

The right of Harrie Williams to be identified as the Author of this Work has been has been asserted by her in accordance with the Copyright, Designs and Patents Act 1988.

All rights reserved.

First published in 2023.

All characters in this publication are entirely fictitious and any resemblance to real persons, living or dead, is purely coincidental.

ISBN: 9798392680719

DEDICATION

To my mum and my sister.
And the cat.

Contents

Prolouge 1
17th August 1979 1
The Beginning Of Time 4
PART 1 7
   Chapter 1 8
      2nd October 2019 8
   Chapter 2 15
      15th July 2011 15
   CHAPTER 3 21
      4th October 2019 21
      7th October 2019 33
      12th October 2019 44
      16th July 2011 54
      22nd July 2011 56
   Chapter 8 60
      16t October 2019 60
      16th October 2019 64
   Chapter 10 72
      20th October 2019 72
   Chapter 11 83
      27th October 2019 83
   Chapter 12 90
      28th October 2019 90

Chapter 13 96
    6th November 2019 96
PART 2 101
    Chapter 1 102
        26/11/2019 102
        17th August 1979 103
    Chapter 2 106
        26/11/2019 106
        March 1983 107
    Chapter 3 110
        26/11/2019 110
        September 1990 111
    Chapter 4 115
        26/11/2019 115
        August 2003 116
    Chapter 5 121
        26/11/2019 121
        May 2010 122
    Chapter 6 126
        26/11/2019 126
        December 2014 126
PART 3 136
    Chapter 1 137
        16th January 2013 137

Chapter 2 143
    22nd July 2011.. 143
Chapter 3 146
    16th October 2019 146
Chapter 4 152
    14th September 2019 152
Chapter 5 157
    17th October 2019 157
PART 4 163
Chapter 1 164
    9:15 – The Dunkeany Residence 164
    10:00 - The Morris Residence 168
Chapter 2 171
    10:00 - Corbeck Town 171
    10:15 - The Morris Residence 172
Chapter 3 175
    17th August 1979 - The Morris Residence 175
Chapter 4 180
    25th November 2019 - 10:40 180
    The Morris Residence 180
Chapter 5 185
    11:30 - The Dunkeany Residence 185
Chapter 6 191
    11:30 – Westgate Train Yard 191

Chapter 7 196
　12:00 - The Morris Residence 196
　12:55 - Outskirts Of The Morris Estate 202
　13:03 - The Morris Estate 203
　30 Minutes Prior - Westgate Train Yard 204
Chapter 8 208
　13:01 The Morris Estate 208
Chapter 9 215
　14:00 – The Morris Residence 215
Chapter 10 220
　25th December 2019 - The Dunkeany Residence ... 220
More By This Author 224

ESSENCE

ACKNOWLEDGMENTS

Thank you to all the readers who pushed through the various drafts of this novel, and provided feedback and particularly spelling and grammar corrections (if there's any mistakes now, it's your fault!)
In particular, thank you to Kat who created this book cover and brought my terrible drawing ideas to life.

PROLOUGE
17TH AUGUST 1979

Westgate trainyard is on fire.

The shells of the empty goods carriages slump inwards in the intense heat, the iron rails holding their wheels warping as the sleepers char. The metal creaks and clunks as it expands in the raging temperatures, competing with the roaring of the flames. It almost drowns out the cries of the man collapsed in the centre of the yard. Almost.

The forest's blaze can be seen from the town, licking above the tips of the trees as billows of smoke vanish into the wide expanse of the night sky. They merge with the thunderous clouds that are hanging heavily over the evening.

Following the train tracks to the south away from the flames of the fire, one is led to the Morris household. As the air clears of smoke, the atmosphere remains warm and oppressive. The tracks terminate at a small holding on the edge of their land, a small receiver of coal and other goods. After the destruction of the fire, several years into the future this access point to the estate is blocked up by a seven-foot wall surrounding the perimeter.

ESSENCE

Although the flames are far behind, there is still noise permeating the atmosphere. A shrill scream of a siren disrupts the eerie stillness. They are racing towards the Morris household, coasting on the first reports of Nathaniel Morris' murder.

Nathaniel himself is responsible for the murder of hundreds of thousands in the war that is currently raging across the sea. He is a leader, a creator, the orchestrator of countless deaths. Many argue his death is deserved, oblivious to the rumours that had been circulating for the past months. That Nathaniel was repenting after his brother's return from war, that he was seeking to reverse the damage he had caused.

A young man, barely seventeen, encounters the blaring police cars and ambulances as he drives through the night. He is pulled aside by a frustratingly thorough police officer. As he unfolds from the driver's seat, the officer is already holding his hand out, "Identity?"

The boy's true identity is one of a thousand eyes, but he hands over the false ID easily. He takes in the officer before him, an Officer Thackery, appreciating the name as he rolls it around the back of his mind. He stores it, deep in the recesses of his memory, for future use.

The boy responds smoothly with his lies, but the officer is stubborn, suspicious. He refuses to release the boy until he understands why he has been found on this road.

The boy grows tired of the questioning, turning to the orange glow saturating the horizon. He gestures to the false dawn, "Do you smell smoke?"

The officer baulks, but the flames still fail to dissuade him of his investigation of the young boy found on the route to a murder scene. The boy grows more exasperated, a tic itching at his eye as he clenches his jaw in frustration.

He toys with the idea. He smiles. He decides it is possible to get away with it.

The boy places a friendly hand on the officer's shoulder. He feels the sparking currents of the officer's neurons beneath his fingers, and he guides and re-directs them playfully. The officer is no longer in control of his own body. He is led back towards his patrol car, guided calmly into the seat. As he unwillingly places his hands on the steering wheel, the boy clenches his fist.

Officer Thackery's heart stops abruptly.

He sits, dead, in the driver's seat. Later, it is determined to be an unexpected heart attack.

The boy returns to his own car, his nonchalant whistling an ugly contrast against the muffled noise of the sirens. He leaves the town of Corbeck.

He returns thirty years later.

THE BEGINNING OF TIME

Eons ago, bestowed upon the human race the ability to manipulate and control matter. This power was gifted in many forms, a flick of a wrist could create a wall of sound through vibrations, or a breath could redirect an air current. The powers became the stuff of legends, of folklore and fairy tales. The Irish Púca, and the infamous werewolves, simply shapeshifters. Nymphs of the water were only humans with the ability to hold a bubble of air below the surface. Yuki-onna, of the Japanese folklore, was a young pale girl with the ability to drop temperatures. Will-o'-the-wisps nothing but cruel pranks of young boys who could create pockets of light.

Humanity basked in their powers. They cultivated them, honoured them, revelled in them. In feudal Japan, the celebrated tradition of Chikara emerged: duels between young men who needed a way of earning respect and honour, or settling an argument. They trained themselves, weaponizing their abilities to perfection. They were rare and dangerous events, but celebrated.

As humanity evolved into the modern era, the fearful tales of their dark histories were rapidly forgotten. They named, studied, and categorised these abilities. Those who could manipulate physical matter became known as Kinaesthetics. Those with the capability of reading and altering emotions were coined as Emotive Abstractions, reflecting the conceptual nature of their power. As new abilities evolved and developed, the list of names grew ever longer.

However, as the concept of Chikara travelled across continents, it quickly mutated into something ugly. Battles were based on bets and gambling. It was not long before these battles were deemed illegal. Arguments were settled with words opposed to the unpredictable, emotionally fuelled battle of Chikara.

Yet, the stories and legends surrounding these battles continued and became a part of adolescent culture. A poor man's version was developed in school yards across the world. Despite teachers attempting to stamp it out, students pushed their own versions of Chikara to settle arguments and heated debates. Usually, these were weak battles as the students did not train like the warriors of Japan and so they did not last long even if they were undiscovered by the school faculty. Horror stories were perpetuated by school districts, of unintentional deaths and mutilations of one student to another, in an attempt to discourage the activity.

Society evolved around these abilities. It established its own routine, normalising one's ability and discouraging the training and weaponizing of it. As a result, abilities weakened through the generations. However, from time to time, a mixing of bloodlines would occur, creating a generation of uniquely powerful abilities. Within this generation, a fearful ability can emerge. One that could control and alter living, organic matter.

The anticipated danger of Organic Kinaesthetics plagued governments for years as they struggled to determine the best course of action. Endless discussion and arguments results in the 'Organic Kinaesthetic Registry'. The registry and its subsequent departments were used to maintain a watchful eye over these rare beings.

ESSENCE

The following records document the occasion when an Organic Kinaesthetic went undetected.

Part 1

Travis and Poppy

ESSENCE

CHAPTER 1
2nd October 2019

Poppy Dunkeany's reverie was broken the instant the insistent rapping on the front door began. She glanced away from the television screen to the clock on the mantel piece. It was ticking relentlessly towards four o'clock. Agatha, her grandmother, continued snoozing, unaware of this intruder into her Wednesday afternoon.

Poppy lay upside down on the sofa, her school uniform rumpled, in an attempt to get the blood flowing to her head. She had the vain hope it would generate some motivation for homework. Her schoolbooks were scattered across the coffee table, despondently waiting to be opened and worked on.

The rapping paused momentarily. Poppy listened, hopeful for the sound of one of her siblings making their way to answer the door. Her twin brother, Aaron, had been thumping restlessly around upstairs. Intermittent slaps and bangs of flying schoolbooks had shaken the ceiling, but now there was silence. There was little chance there then. Maybe Mallory would abandon her search for a snack in the kitchen?

The rapping resumed and she sighed. Hauling herself up,

she rested briefly against the living room door as her body re-distributed her blood, and then pulled the front door open.

"Oh, hi Poppy!" Travis Lee stood on the doorstep, hands thrust nonchalantly into his pockets. He seemed surprised to see her, as if the fact she lived here in the same house as her twin was unexpected.

"Hi Travis," Poppy stood still, clutching the door handle. He wore a forest green sweatshirt, beneath which his crumpled school shirt protruded. This boy was an enigma.

The two of them had been close when they were young. He would theatrically show her his party tricks, changing a daffodil from yellow to blue or their school ties from navy to crimson. The fond memory of the elephant trod slowly into her mind, waving its orange trunk.

But close on the heels of that memory was the discovery of her own powerlessness. He had drifted seamlessly into the pitying school crowd, choosing her brother's friendship over hers.

She was unsure whether she had ever forgiven him for that.

"When was the last time we spoke?" she asked pointedly, attempting to disguise her feelings with an awkward, nostalgic smile.

He ran a hand through his dark curls, scratching the back of his head as he tried to answer, "I don't know," he shrugged, "It's been a while, hasn't it?"

She restrained herself from answering the question, "What do you want?" she abruptly asked. Nobody knocked on doors anymore. You awkwardly wait at the end of your friend's drive until they read your message of arrival, at which point said friend would meet you. None of this nonsense of knocking on doors.

Unless, of course, you didn't have their phone number, Poppy thought. For example, if you hadn't spoken for a while and knocking on their door was the only way to reconnect...

"I've been waiting for Aaron," he interrupted her thought

flow, showing her several unread messages to her brother on his cracked phone screen, "But he's not answered,"

Turning away, unable to hide the blush of embarrassment on her face, she yelled her brother's name.

Aaron's door opened upstairs, squealing on its hinges, and he appeared at the top of the stairs in his boxers. His hair was flattened on one side, and his face was pink. He saw Travis and groaned, "Man, I fell asleep,"

Poppy flung the door open so Travis could enter, "You might as well come in, he needs to get dressed," As if that weren't already obvious.

"I'll be ten minutes," Aaron called, slamming his bedroom door shut.

Travis wiped his feet and uncomfortably sidled into the living room, perhaps picking up on Poppy's growing animosity towards him. He perched on the edge of the sofa that she had been sprawled across minutes earlier.

Mallory's face peered out from the kitchen at the end of the hall, her dark hair scraped back into braids in preparation for her netball trials, "You gonna offer him a drink or anything?" she hissed. Poppy admired her sister for many reasons: her intelligence, her penchant for sport, her prettiness. Her nagging was not one of them.

"Of course!" Poppy retorted, jutting her chin out, despite the fact that she actually had no intention. Ex-best friends who ditch you don't deserve manners. Unfortunately, Travis had heard Mallory and requested a glass of water. Poppy flounced into the kitchen, found the smallest glass tumbler she could, and filled it halfway with lukewarm water. Mallory failed to notice, already pouring over her schoolwork at the kitchen island.

Fully aware of her own pettiness, Poppy returned to the living room to find Travis cautiously watching her grandmother. Agatha had woken up and had begun to knit. The ball of yarn kept floating away from her and she kept having to claw it back from its weightless adventure with arthritic fingers.

ESSENCE

"Harrison, could you be a dear and hold this?" she asked Travis, her Irish accent buried beneath the roughness of her voice.

He froze in confusion, glancing around the room as if someone named Harrison may leap from behind the sofa.

"She has dementia," Poppy explained from the doorway, "You'll have to excuse her, she probably thinks you're someone else,"

"I know exactly who that is," Agatha retorted stubbornly, "It's Harrison Lee! Please could you hold this dear?"

Travis sprang to his feet and held the ball of yarn firmly. "I'm not Harrison," he corrected her, "I'm his son, Travis,"

Agatha continued knitting as if she had not heard him, "How is that lovely Morris girl of yours?" she asked sweetly.

Poppy held the glass of water out to Travis, but he shrugged helplessly. She poured it into her avocado plant instead, taking one of the leaves gently between two fingers. It was brightening up now, much improved from its droopy state this morning.

She sent it her 'growing thoughts'. It was a small habit she had developed years ago when she was a child. She had been small when she had started gardening, and she remembered all those times she had spent with her mother, speaking to the plants, and encouraging them to grow. She still did it even now, although no longer out loud. She knew it had no consequence at all, but it had made it easier when she lost a plant, believing she had given it all she could.

"We got married," Travis was saying, playing along with Agatha now, "We had a son,"

Poppy settled on the arm of the sofa, opposite her Grandmother's chair. Agatha was rarely lucid these days, she was losing against her dementia. She commonly lost herself in memories of her childhood and her own folktales. She rarely remembered her grandchildren's names now, although she had yet to forget her love for them.

"That's lovely!"

"Yeah, he's called Travis,"

ESSENCE

Her face pulled taut briefly, a sign of dislike, "A rather modern name," she managed.
There was a brief silence before she asked again, "How is that lovely Morris girl of yours?"
Poppy sighed, "Gran, this is Travis," she tried.
"I've forgotten her name," Agatha continued, a worried frown wrinkling her forehead.
"Anna," Travis supplied.
"Anna Morris," Agatha rolled the name around her mouth, the frown deepening, "Has she made up with her mother?"
Travis seemed to stiffen, the ball of yarn pinching between his fingertips, "Uh..."
Poppy sensed that this innocent, confused conversation driven by her grandmother had strayed into an unknown, sensitive territory. She opened her mouth to distract her when Agatha's arm thrust out gripped Travis' wrist.
"She's no good Harrison," she hissed, "No good," The knitting needles continued to jaggedly knit, spearing the crocheted yarn. Poppy's schoolbooks began to fumble awkwardly upwards, floating precariously in the air. Poppy hastily grabbed them, thrusting them beneath the leg of the coffee table.
"Gran!" she raised her voice, "Agatha!"
"No good Harrison!"
"Who's no good?" Travis demanded.
The ball of yarn in his grip began to pulsate, shifting colours in kaleidoscopic ripples. The situation was rapidly spiralling out of Poppy's control. She struggled to handle her Grandmother's episodes, especially when everything began moving and the sticky tape holding the ornaments to the mantle began to peel away.
She shouted for Mallory, her voice pitching with stress. She tried to pry Agatha's hand from Travis' wrist, but the arthritic fingers seemed locked in place.
"She drives the Coiste Bodhar!" Agatha hissed.
"Mallory!" she called more desperately.
Mallory thundered in, followed by Aaron. She swore at the

sight, loose items twirled haphazardly in the air, objects touching Travis pulsated through a spectrum of colours, like rainbow Jellyfish. Poppy was shaking, her hands fluttering between prying her grandmother off Travis and trying to catch floating objects.

Mallory knelt in front of her grandmother and took her firmly by the shoulders, "Agatha," she said gently, "Can you look at me please?"

Agatha's focus shifted from Travis to Mallory. The objects stilled in the air. Poppy and Aaron quickly gathered the most fragile ones.

"Thank you, Agatha. I think you're feeling a bit confused, aren't you? But that's okay, we all feel a bit confused sometimes. I'm here to help you,"

Agatha relaxed, her fingers loosening. Travis pulled his hand away, dropping the yarn at his feet. He stumbled back, anxiously rubbing his wrist. The remaining objects, the TV remote, a loose slipper, and a takeaway menu fell to the ground as Mallory continued soothingly talking to her grandmother.

"Gran?" Aaron murmured.

"I... I don't..." Agatha stuttered, frowning at him.

Mallory glared at him over her shoulder, "Out, all of you,"

They all silently filed from the living room, and Poppy pulled the door shut behind them. She turned to a pale Travis, "Look, I'm really sorry about that. Sometimes she has these episodes, and they can get a bit out of control," the words stumbled over themselves in their hurry to leave her mouth.

"We should be going," Aaron interrupted bluntly, pulling a jacket on.

Travis led himself be tugged away, but Poppy rested a hand on his arm, "Seriously, we're sorry. I saw that some of the things she said upset you, but she meant nothing by it,"

Travis managed a smile, "It's okay. Don't worry, I get it," Her hand slipped off his sweater and Aaron tugged him through the front door. It was as he was closing it behind

him that Travis paused and turned back to Poppy.
"We should catch up some time,"
She blinked in surprise and stood stupidly silent for a moment.
"I mean, if you want to," he prompted.
"Yeah," she finally responded hoarsely, "That would be nice,"
Poppy watched Travis walk away with her brother down the street. He was taller than Aaron now. She thought of young Travis who was clumsy and uncoordinated, who used to slouch. She wondered if he remembered the orange elephant too.

CHAPTER 2
15th July 2011

The Dunkeanys settled themselves awkwardly into the little plastic chairs designed for eight-year-olds. Claire glanced at her husband Patrick and they shared a knowing smile as they looked towards their children's teacher, perched above them on the only adult chair in the room.

The couple were attending Poppy and Aaron's parents' evening. They sat in a classroom plastered with their children's scribbled artworks and prayers. Pots of coloured pencils lined the windowsill, and several jars of coloured water held stalks of celery.

The teacher noticed Patrick staring confusedly at them, "They're a science experiment," she gestured, "to highlight the water transportation systems within a plant,"

Patrick nodded blankly.

"Let's get started," the teacher smiled through her exhaustion. This was the last couple of the night, she was looking forward to going home, "My name is Ellen Davies, I am the main teacher for both Aaron and Poppy. They are both simply lovely children," She leaned over and pulled a wad of papers from her bag. She flicked through them, and finally found the work she was looking for.

"Let's start with Aaron. He is definitely a… precocious young boy, and he is intelligent, but he struggles to apply this intelligence to his schoolwork. As you can see here," she pointed to a question on a test sheet, "He has got the right answer, but has failed to show his workings,"

"Why's that a problem?" Patrick asked, "If he's getting the right answer?"

"We encourage all students to show their workings so that if they get it wrong, we can work back and find out why," Miss Davies responded stiffly.

"But he got the right answer?"

Claire put a firm hand on his leg, glaring at her husband.

Miss Davies donned her expressionless mask, perfected to hide her short temper, before continuing, "It's a practice we want them to get into," was all she said, "Anyway, Aaron is curious and is popular with his friends, but he does need to work on his attention span, as it is quite… short,"

Claire nodded, thinking of the hours her son could spend glued to the television. She failed to see a lacking attention span there.

"In terms of his abilities, we're seeing a display of kinaesthetic and oral. He can create various sound and physical vibrations, physical being the dominant, to create disturbances. Mostly within my classroom!" she laughed forcefully. Claire could see pain in her eyes.

"What about our Poppy?" Patrick asked.

Miss Davies straightened the papers on her desk with her fingertips as she considered the question, "She produces her schoolwork to a good standard," she began, "She is not the most outstanding of students, but she most certainly isn't falling behind either,"

The Dunkeany's waited, anxiously frozen in their too small seats as Miss Davies paused again. Claire tugged at the loose threads on the sleeve of her cardigan, confused and stressed by the teacher's reluctance to speak.

"If I'm honest," Miss Davies sighed, "I have some

concerns. She appears disconnected from the reality around her," she sounded as if she was quoting someone, her eyes drifting as she recalled the phrase.

"You see here," she pulled out the image of a crudely drawn elephant, clumsily scribbled in the colour orange, "This is a perfect example of how Poppy neglects the accuracy of her reality. Of course, this was okay in infants, but she has failed to grow out of it like the rest of the children have. She is easily distracted, telling tales of banshees and butterflies and mermaids. She scares the other children,"

"My mother is Irish," Patrick explained, "She tells the children stories from her folklore, the same stories she told me," he added testily.

Ellen Davies pursed her lips, "It needs to stop,"

She pulled another sheet from her stack of papers. Upon it was a pencil drawing of a landscape, sketched over the worksheet questions beneath, "This is the worksheet from our trip to the National Library last month," Miss Davies said, "As you can see, Poppy has completely disregarded the worksheet. In fact, she completely disregarded each and every workshop arranged for the children that day. We were exploring the culture and construction of our history in what I thought were engaging methods for the children. Such as the Barovian War and other major events. But Poppy insisted on a 'bigger picture' to look at," Miss Davies emphasised her point by twitching her fingers in the form of air quotes, "I can only imagine she meant the view,"

"Did you talk to her about it?" Claire asked. She stared in confusion at the worksheet. The older Poppy got, she realised, the less she understood her. She glanced at her husband, his brow furrowed in consternation.

"We did. She failed to understand the importance of this work, and of course, it's unfair on the other children for us to be seen as treating her any differently. She finished the work to a minimum standard throughout her morning breaktimes the following week,"

"Is there anything we can do?" Patrick tried, "She obviously isn't responding well to this kind of learning,"

"She's just a little different, that's all," Claire agreed.

"More than you realise," Miss Davies smiled sadly, "I'm afraid there has been no indication of any form of ability expressed by your daughter Mr and Mrs Dunkeany,"

Miss Davies continued talking, explaining the procedure for those children who lack any form of ability manifestation. The support that was available for Poppy's physical and mental wellbeing in light of this discovery. Miss Davies suggested a friend of hers, Dr. Clarence Thackery, as a guidance counsellor of sorts to help Poppy adjust to her lack of power. She could undergo tests for confirmation, but Miss Davies did not hold much hope.

The Dunkeany's heard little of this. Their minds were brimming with visions of their daughter growing up a pariah, excluded from so many things in her future, all because she was powerless.

...

"The sea stretches, it stretches so far that you cannot see where it ends and where the sky begins. The horizon is invisible!" Agatha Dunkeany smiled at the young, captivated faces before her. Finally dressed in pyjamas and ready for bed, she was treating her three grandchildren to a story before she ushered them upstairs. Her son and daughter-in-law had yet to return from their parents' evening at school, so she had taken advantage of the extra time.

"I was standing on the golden beach," she continued, the lilt of Irish in her voice lulling the children into an entranced stupor, "It was May time. The sun was glorious, warm on my face, but the ocean was still icy cold, holding onto the winter's chill. So, you can imagine my surprise when a woman emerges from the water!"

The children gasped.

"All she was dressed in was a slip of silk and sixteen-year-old me couldn't believe my eyes! She was beautiful! She had long dark curls and deep, dark pools for eyes. She wasn't shivering, she didn't look the slightest bit cold despite standing waist deep in the water! I realised then and there that she must have been a mermaid, not a merrow with their piggy face and sharp teeth, but a real-life mermaid!"

The children could not hide their excitement, it emerged in suppressed giggles, shining eyes and clenched fists. The click of a key turning in the lock is only heard by Agatha. She realised she did not have much time left.

"Suddenly, I find myself walking towards her! I can't stop my legs from moving, I join her in the sea. Water is frothing around me and my clothes are wet but I don't care! I'm standing in front of a mermaid! Then she says to me, she says, 'My dearest Agatha, you look so beautiful' and she looks so sad, 'How is your father?'

"I tell her he is not doing well; he's been ill for a few months up until that point you see, and I honestly cannot describe the look of pain that crossed her features. She says to me then, 'I stayed with you father for many months. I loved him. And out of that love came you.'"

"What does that mean?" a voice interrupted from the floor.

"It means, Aaron my boy, it means she was my mother. I had a mermaid for a mother!"

Coats and shoes can be heard from the hallway, as both Patrick and Claire noisily come home. The children have tensed, conscious that their story time is nearly over.

"So, my mother, the mermaid, she holds my hands and tells me how proud she is of me. How much she loves me and my Da. Then it is time for her to go and she kisses me gently on my forehead. And that is how I became pregnant with your Da. She gifted me my own babe,"

"Those are some pretty wild tales, Ma," Patrick interrupted softly from the doorway, "Come on kids, bedtime,"

With much grumbling, the children shifted themselves. They would believe that story for several months, that babies were made by the kiss of a mermaid. That is, until Mallory sat through her first biology lesson on sexual reproduction and learnt the harrowing truth. It had nothing to do with mermaids at all.

As Claire settled the children down, Patrick sat with his mother. He explained to Agatha that Poppy's teacher told them she should no longer tell the children her stories. That the tales are confusing them.

"Don't be ridiculous Paddy!" Agatha scolded, "I told you all those stories and you turned out just fine!"

"Poppy's powerless Ma," Patrick blurted gloomily.

Silence pervaded the room. The significance of the statement hung heavily over the pair. It became too much for Agatha, the tears welled in her eyes before she could stop them.

"Oh son, I saw the pooka. I saw him and I have brought bad luck on your house," She buried her face in her hands, already papery and brittle.

Unable to move, Patrick could only watch. He worried for his mother, there were signs of illness in her mind. The fact she was seeing the very creatures from her own stories only consolidated the fact.

"Agatha?" Claire called from the kitchen, "Why are there peas on the stove?"

Flushed, Agatha looked up confused, "Peas?"

Claire entered the living room, a pan of peas boiled dry in her hands, "Did you not give the peas to the kids?"

Agatha glanced between her son and his wife, bewildered. She looked, in Patrick's mind, heartbreakingly old and fragile.

"The pooka," she sighed sadly.

CHAPTER 3
4th October 2019

Travis Lee pulled his tie loose and shook the foggy thoughts of his maths class from his mind as he clattered down the front steps of school. He had agreed to meet Poppy at the front gate after the final lesson of the day. He was surprised she had said yes to him the other day, especially after the cold shoulder she had given him when he had first arrived.

He had considered Poppy a close friend when they were younger. But then the diagnosis had happened, and it had scared him. He was scared she would hate him for having powers, that she would be jealous. He found he didn't want to use his powers around her, felt guilty that he had something she would never have. He could only pity her and could no longer find the words to speak to her when there was this great, gaping chasm of difference between them.

But then they had so many classes together that year and it had become so clear to him. She simply did not care. She wasn't bothered by the difference between her and everyone else. It always seemed that she had more important things on her mind when she was gazing out the window during class, whilst the teacher suppressed the disrupting powers of everyone else in the room.

Travis only noticed the man watching him because he was searching for Poppy in the crowd. He was old; his scraggly hair was grey and his beard held several weeks of uninhibited growth. His clothes were dirty and stained. Large hands in fingerless gloves emerged from the long sleeves of the overcoat he wore to combat the cool October air. Stark blue eyes were watching him steadily from the stern, wrinkled face that hid beneath the battered red beanie.

Travis felt his heart jump erratically within his ribcage. It lurched forward with sudden fear, like it used to when he mistook his dressing gown for an intruder in the dark of the night. Who was this man? Why was he watching him so intently? He surreptitiously searched around for another possible student the man could be watching. But Travis himself was the only one waiting at the school gates. He felt a shiver slide sinisterly up his spine as a sense of familiarity grew in his mind.

The thought was broken, however, by a slap between his shoulder blades. Travis stumbled forwards at the unexpected force and when he looked up again, the man was gone.

"Lee,"

"Dunkeany," Travis responded to Aaron's shoulder slap with a punch of his own. Their friends, Mikey Lewis and Benjamin Nobel, followed closely behind.

"Looks like you scared him there, Dunkeany," Mikey grinned, bouncing on the balls of his feet. His big brown eyes roved between the two of them from beneath the worn cap he always wore.

"No way," Travis retorted.

Benji placed a reassuring hand on Travis' shoulder, "Feels like you're worried about something,"

Travis shrugged him off. He didn't want Benji sensing the fear that had just enveloped him. There was no way he could explain it, he failed to understand it himself.

"You worried about tonight?" Aaron demanded.

Travis shook his head, "I'm not coming tonight,"

"Why not?"

"I've got a thing," Travis lied lamely. He doubted using Aaron's sister as an excuse for missing tonight would go down well.

Mikey stopped bouncing, "A thing?" he repeated incredulously, "A more important thing?"

Travis felt the air around his ears begin to vibrate and a building pressure on his temples, "Oh don't get pissed Dunkeany," he moaned, shoving Aaron's shoulder, "Knock it off,"

The pressure faded. Aaron nodded, as if satisfied.

"Whatever, we can practice some things without you," he said, "But need you tomorrow man,"

"Yeah, I'll be there tomorrow," Travis muttered, "And Aaron?" he called as the three boys walked away from him, "Do that again and I'll permanently turn you blue,"

Aaron threw back his head as he guffawed, "Alright Lee, sure,"

"I think looking like a smurf will suit you," Benji added. Blonde hair flopped in his face as he looked at Aaron with a grin.

"You think?"

As their voices faded, Travis once again began searching the diminishing crowd of students for Poppy. Every now and then, he would glance towards the side of the road where the man had stood, but there was no sign of him.

But suddenly there was Poppy! She had emerged from the thinning crowd and had gripped her brother by the elbow. Her face was screwed up as she demanded something. They were too far away for him to hear what they were saying. She only became more frustrated at Aaron's laugh and apparent lack of appreciation of the seriousness of her question. Mikey danced around them, his endless amounts of energy expressed as bad jokes and strong air currents that ruffled all their hair. Benji was Mikey's opposite, he stood patiently still whilst the breeze brushed his hair from his forehead, revealing his countless freckles. Usually so neutral, his face reflected Poppy's frustration.

Poppy eventually let her brother go and strode over to Travis, her blonde hair flowing in wisps around her head, "Do you know where he's going? He keeps disappearing, is he dating someone or something?" She stared suspiciously at the retreating figure of her brother and his two friends. Aaron threw an arm around Benji's shoulders as the three of them took the turn leading to Westgate Forest.

"I have no idea," Travis shrugged. Actually, he had every idea. But the four of them had made a pact.

"So where do you want to go? I have a history project that was due today that I haven't started, so a table would be ideal," the late afternoon sunlight washed over her, making her hair and skin glow as she looked expectantly at him.

"Uh, Maisie's has tables," he suggested, "And milkshakes?"

"Tables and milkshakes," she smiled, "Sounds good,"

They began walking, shoulder to shoulder, away from the school gates as Travis asked, "When's it due?"

"Tomorrow,"

"How are you supposed to hand in homework on a Saturday?"

"I'm expected to email it," Poppy rolled her eyes.

She began complaining about her history teacher when Travis saw him again. The man. He stood in the shadow of an oak, glaring coldly at him. Travis fearfully held his gaze and jumped slightly when Poppy tugged at his sleeve.

She looked hurt, "Are you listening?"

"Am I...? Of course I am!" he responded indignantly, glancing back at the shadow of the tree. Again, the man was gone, but Travis could not shake the feeling he was being watched.

Poppy followed his gaze to the empty space beneath the tree, and looked at him with confusion, "Are you alright?"

"Yeah, 'course," he reassured her, "Can we just move a bit faster, it's pretty cold out here,"

They hurried along the road. Brown and orange leaves were scattered wetly along the pavement. Travis felt his trainers slip several times on the slick ground. The trees that populated the street still had some leaves clinging to their skeletal branches. October had arrived unexpectedly quickly; the Autumnal season had swept in with relentless rain and bracing winds.

Maisie's squatted on the corner of the main high street. It was a wannabe retro-diner. Neon lights affronted the eyes as you entered, clashing with the red and white checked cloths on the tables and the chess-board styling of the floor. But the seats were comfortable, and they served decent food and milkshakes. And it had tables.

Travis' trainers squeaked on the floor as they walked to the counter to order. He felt safer inside, surrounded by the bellowing juke box and bright lights. He glanced nervously one last time through the glass front of the diner, but there was no sign of the mysterious stranger.

Poppy ordered a salted caramel shake that arrived at their table dripping with cream and sauce. Travis ordered a 'Berry Blitz', drenched in end-of-season raspberries and strawberries. The waitress delivered their drinks with a side of classic small talk, "It's a shame how quickly it gets dark now!" she commented, "Winter is on its way,"

"I feel like that's all people say now," Poppy whispered as the waitress floated away, "Even though it happens every year, everyone is still so surprised!"

The pair had chosen a table in the corner, as far from the juke box as possible so that they could actually hear one another talk. Poppy started chatting as soon as they had taken their seats. She apologised again for the way her Grandmother had acted when he had visited. She mentioned that she was sad that they had not spoken in so long, but she was happy to see him doing so well.

"Tell me about your friends," she said eventually.

"Well, I'm pretty sure you know Aaron better than I do," Travis joked, finally settling calmly into his chair. The old stuffing moulded uncomplaining to his back, "Mikey is crazy. We're convinced he's got an IV drip at home that gets him juiced up on energy drinks. Benji is quieter, shyer. Thinks more before he talks,"

"What about their abilities? Aaron doesn't talk much about them, but Mikey is an air current kinaesthetic right?"

It was a common enough question. An ability was an indicator of a person's personality, a physical manifestation of who they were. It was far more suspicious for a person to dodge the question. Hiding your ability was akin to wearing a mask. It was for criminals.

Travis had, however, deliberately neglected to bring their abilities up in fear of upsetting Poppy, "You really wanna hear about that?"

Poppy tilted her head and smiled knowingly, "What? Because I don't have any powers, you think it would upset me?"

He struggled to answer. That had been his exact thought. It was incomprehensible to him that someone who was powerless would want to know what they were missing out on.

"You did think that!" she accused, reading his expression easily.

"I'm sorry, I didn't mean-"

"Don't be sorry," she snapped, interrupting him, "It's a stupid assumption. It's like you never wanting to talk about birds because you can't fly," The words burst out of her in a tidal wave.

"I didn't think of it like that," he meekly took a sip of his drink.

"No, nobody does," Poppy reached into her bag and pulled out her history project. She spread out some papers on the desk and began scribbling at the top of the page. The scratching of her pen was the only noise to break the suddenly tense silence.

"I would still be interested to hear what they are like though," she mumbled to the page.

Travis didn't look up as he sipped from his milkshake, "Mikey is a kinaesthetic with air currents," he said quietly, "he can control the molecules to create breezes. Half the time he does this without realising. Benji is an emotive abstraction. He can feel other people's feelings,"

She glanced up from her scribbling, "That must be hard,"

"Yeah, he gets tired a lot," In addition to that, it was taboo for Benji and others like him to make non-consensual skin-on-skin contact with anyone. Travis, Mikey and Aaron tolerated it to an extent, conscious that Benji struggled with his power and the unspoken laws that went with it.

She finally stopped writing and looked at him again. He found himself unable to look away from her face. Her eyes sat big and round and beautifully in her pale face. She rested her chin in the palm of her hand and blinked in the heavy sunlight that drifted directly into her face. She looked golden again.

"And you can change the colour of things," she said.

Travis grinned and touched the tip of her pen. It flickered and turned purple. She tried to draw a purple heart, but the ink quickly faded back to black again when he let go.

"How does that work?"

"Chromatophores," he answered, "I can manipulate them, and have my own store of them,"

"Do you think you'll ever run out?"

His face dropped. The thought had never occurred to him, "I assumed I generated them rather than having a stockpile," He tried to swirl his milkshake with the straw, but the paper had started disintegrating. He pulled it free of the drink and stared sadly at the drooping straw.

Poppy nodded and took a slurp of her milkshake before turning back to her work.

"What is the history project about?" Travis asked, desperate to clear his mind of the possibility that his ability might run itself dry someday.

"Turning points in Corbeck's history,"

"Sounds dull,"

"It is. Not my choice though. There are no turning points or anything of significance in our history,"

"What about Nathaniel Morris?"

"Everyone is doing that," Poppy rolled her eyes

"Even his murder?"

She paused and frowned, "Morris murder," she murmured. Travis watched her mind work as she tried to place the name, "Wasn't he related to you?" she asked.

He smiled at her bluntness. He had discovered throughout his life that most people avoided the topic of his grandfather. Even his own mother.

"Uh huh, he was my grandfather. Invented the Morris Mios, frontier of chemical warfare. Made a major impact in the Barovian War. It's a marmite kind of situation,"

"Wow, I had no idea he was murdered,"

Travis laughed, "Me neither! Not until a few years ago. He died a long time ago, and we don't visit my Grandmother. Like at all,"

"How come?"

He shrugged. Poppy realised his shoulders had tensed uncomfortably. This was a subject he was not happy to discuss openly.

"Would you mind if I did some research into him?" she asked, "I mean, I'm sure I could find something else if you're not comfortable with it,"

Travis shrugged again, awkwardly scratching the back of his neck, "I don't mind. Maybe you could teach me something new, huh?"

CHAPTER 4
Historical Turning Points – The Mystery of Nathaniel Morris
By Poppy Dunkeany

Introduction

The Morris Mios is the legacy of Nathaniel Morris, a leading chemist and engineer from the late 1960s and early 1970s. There are a great many reasons why Morris played an integral part within Corbeck's history as well as the Barrovian War (1972-1980). However, he was unable to see the true extent of his role due to his untimely and mysterious death in 1978. This essay, with reference to the role he played in the war, will primarily explore his homelife and murder and how this impacted the town.

Context

The Barrovian War lasted eight years (1972-1980) due to an accumulation of animosity between our country and the northern island of Barrovyn. Several years of trade disagreements and civil unrest in Barrovyn accumulated and was ignited into war by the assassination of President Morgan in 1971 (Peters, 1990). Accusations were made of our country supplying Barrovyn terrorists with the weapons involved in the assassination.

As a result, Barrovyn declared war on 19th February 1972.

Morris Miosis - a fore-front of chemical warfare

Morris Miosis, more commonly referred to as Morris Mios, was a newly developed version of the nerve agent Sarin gas. Its name, Miosis, was coined from the characteristic enlargement of the pupil under exposure to it (Matthews, 2000). It was particularly volatile and lethal in its use during the Barrovian War (Peters, 1990) due to the fact that it could be introduced to water sources as well as into ventilation systems and the air in general. Exposure to the chemical would result in:

- Loss of consciousness
- Convulsions
- Paralysis
- Respiratory failure
- Death

These symptoms were rapid and difficult to reverse resulting in as many as 112,000 deaths (Denton, 1988) and countless casualties on both sides. Although at first the gas was widely well received when it was first commercially used in 1974, its use quickly became controversial when the effects of the gas were truly realised. The greatest opponent to its use was Nathaniel's brother, Joseph Morris. After its acquisition from Nathaniel Morris by Io Technologies in 1978, Morris Mios was produced until December 1982, whereas production was made illegal. However, leaked documents in 1990 revealed continued production. This caused irreparable damage to the company's reputation.

The death of Nathaniel Morris - a murder

Nathaniel Morris grew up with a younger brother three years his junior, Joseph. Early reports regarding the two boys told of a secure friendship in their early lives (Karys et al. 2012). Whilst Nathaniel studied for his chemistry degree, Joseph undertook studies in Medicine. He was heavily involved as a doctor in the war effort from 1975, at only 20 years old.

Nathaniel married in the autumn of 1970 at 18 years old to Edith Pickerton, aged 17. Together, they had two children: Anna (1973) and Margaret (1975). Joseph, on the other hand, remained a bachelor as he moved abroad to Barrovyn to care for wounded soldiers.

Joseph returned home after four years in 1977, from the borders of Barrovyn where hospital sites were mostly located. The war had taken thousands of lives and many of those were due to Nathaniel and his nerve agent. As a result, Joseph returned home a disheartened and broken man.

According to sources (Karys et al. 2012; Maple, 1997), Joseph begged Nathaniel to halt production of his nerve agent, but Nathaniel refused for supposed financial reasons. Arguably, these reasons are postulated as there is no direct evidence of Nathaniel's reasoning behind continuation of Mios production. In fact, he elected to sell the company instead of halting production. As a result, Joseph supposedly murdered his brother on the 17th August 1979.

On the night of the murder, several police officers and doctors descended on the scene rapidly. Although rarely noted, there was an officer who was unable to make it to the scene as he suffered a heart attack en route to the scene. The officer's name was not recorded.

Reports from the time regarded Joseph as an "intelligent but empathetic man" who rarely endured the pain and torment of others (Karys et al. 2012). This common knowledge of Joseph's personality was one of the main contradicting aspects of the case, in addition to the Hippocratic Oath sworn by all doctors.

Unfortunately, Joseph disappeared shortly thereafter, and the case could not be brought to trial. There was evidence of him destroying the Westgate trainyard, causing it to fall into disuse and eventually close several years later. His motives behind this attack are unknown.

A formal confession was required for the case to be

closed, as a confession is regarded as one of the most impactful pieces of evidence (Shifton, 2019). However, there was no formal confession nor much evidence (except for the argument overheard by Nathaniel's wife, Edith, and the fact that Joseph was the last person to see Nathaniel alive), the general consensus is that Joseph killed his elder brother.

Conclusion

In conclusion, the unusual and unsolved death of Nathaniel Morris sparked additional controversy to the already prevalent debate of ethics surrounding the use of Morris Mios. The fact that our town is the home of Morris and his descendants is a perfect example of how a person originating from Corbeck has had a major impact on history and can therefore be considered a historical turning point.

Grade: C-

CHAPTER 5
7th October 2019

"So Mallory, did you get the results of the netball trials?" Claire asked as she served her home-grown potatoes. Six plates sat on the counter, already piled high with steaming vegetables. The garden was overflowing with produce again thanks to the devotion of herself and Poppy to it, but she was struggling to find use for it all.

"I've made the team!" Mallory responded, grinning as she cleared her study books from the table.

There was a mumble of affirmative noises from the remaining Dunkeany's sat around the table, patiently awaiting their dinners. Agatha nodded sagely, despite paying little attention to the exchange.

"Please, hold your enthusiasm," Mallory said dryly. She slumped into her seat and flicked her brother's ear, "Did you hear that?"

Aaron grumpily smacked her hand away, "Oh my God, I don't care," he grumbled, finally looking up from his phone.

"What's so important you can't look up from your phone and congratulate your sister?" Patrick asked, hypocritically failing to glance up from his newspaper. He absent-mindedly moulded his fork into varying shapes as he concentrated.

"Says you. Poppy's doing exactly the same," Aaron pouted grumpily.

"Please don't mess with the cutlery Pat," Claire called over from the kitchen.

"Sorry honey," Patrick replaced the fork, in its original form, back on the table, "You know there has been another student Chikara incident in London?" he continued distractedly, "Another death apparently, two kids trying to settle and argument,"

"All those stories are bull," Aaron snorted, "Ofsted make them up to try and stop anyone else from trying it,"

Patrick shrugged and threw the newspaper onto the kitchen counter. It skidded frictionlessly across and off the other side. He chose to ignore his wife's glare and turned to his daughter, "Tell us about netball then,"

"I mean, Naomi told me at lunch today and training is every Wednesday," Mallory shrugged, "There's not a lot to tell,"

"You've wasted all our time," Aaron sighed.

"You already waste your time," Mallory retorted.

"I don't actually, I'm very productive,"

Patrick harshly shushed the bickering siblings, suddenly distracted by the sound of the radio. The voices crackled distinctly against the white noise of static.

"In the midst of the Chikara championships, which will be finishing with the penultimate fight next Wednesday, tragedy has once again struck. A fourteen-year-old girl has died after being involved in an illegal Chikara battle yesterday,"

"This is what I just read about," Patrick waved his hand eagerly.

"Accusations have arisen in regards to whether the excessive publication of Chikara in the media and in the recent championships has encouraged inexperienced youth to attempt these dangerous battles,"

"It's just terrible," Patrick shook his head, but his words still fell short of expressing the gravity of the situation.

Mallory paled to a sickly pallor, "Fourteen?"

"I'm glad none of you are involved in this sort of thing," Claire murmured.

"What would you do if I wanted to be?" Aaron asked tentatively.

"Eh?" Patrick stared at his son as if he had never seen him before.

"Like professionally?"

"Don't be stupid!" Mallory interjected hotly.

"I'm not!"

"Don't you know how dangerous that is?" Mallory prodded her brother with a fingertip, deliberately giving him a faint electric shock.

"Hey!" Aaron smacked his hand on the table, focusing the vibrations to the base of Mallory's glass of water. It jumped, splashing water onto her lap.

Mallory leapt to her feet. "Oh, you idiot! If you can't handle a little electric shock, you definitely can't handle a Chikara!"

"Do not shock your brother!" Patrick scolded.

"Dad!" Mallory gaped, angrily gesturing at Aaron, furious at the unfairness of being singled out.

Glancing upwards, Poppy was amused to see the lightbulb centred above their heads begin to flicker as Mallory's anger urged the movement of electrons. The microwave beeped, the kettle briefly switched on, and the radio blared loudly before suddenly dying.

"Mallory!"

"How come I'm the scape goat in this?" she demanded. Leaping at Aaron, her palm fizzed as she reached out to touch him. With a flick of the wrist, Patrick gathered all the cutlery, combining it into a flat sheet of metal. He flung it forwards, intercepting Mallory's sparking fingers. The electricity crackled through the sheet, scattering, and merging again in Mallory's fingertips. She shrieked at her own shock.

Aaron saw his opportunity. He smacked the sheet firmly with the palm of his hand. Vibrations reverberated as it smacked into his sister. Agatha jumped and gasped, and several other glasses on the table sprang into the air, spilling their contents. Patrick swore, annoyed he had not managed to catch it in time. He launched to his feet, pulling the sheet away and grabbing Aaron by his shirt collar. Mallory leapt forwards again, energy crackling.

"Please!" Claire's voice rang out against the fighting like white lightning against a dark sky, "Can you have some decency? Some sensitivity?" she demanded.

An awkward silence descended. Mallory slumped back into her seat as Aaron gathered paper towels to clean up the mess. They both glanced sheepishly at their sister. Patrick humbly separated the metal out into knives and forks, but they did not look quite as they did before.

"I hope you're not all looking at me," Poppy interrupted the silence without glancing up from her phone. She was conscious of her mother's need to protect her from the smallest presentation of powers around her. It was in every gesture, every word, every huff, and sigh whenever Claire saw someone displaying their abilities unnecessarily. It was the endless sessions of therapy that Poppy had to endure.

But she couldn't care less that she was powerless. She had never known any different. Her siblings always fought using theirs. Her peers at school would constantly manipulate matter when the teacher turned away. She understood that most people were born with varying abilities to manipulate their environment. She had no intention of playing the pity card and stopping them to save her own feelings.

Each member of the Dunkeany family pretended they were resting their sight on something completely different to Poppy. A chair leg, the herbs on the kitchen windowsill, a big toe protruding from a hole in a sock.

"Of course not sweetie," Claire reassured her, glaring at

the rest of the family as she brought steaming plates of casserole and potato to the table, "Phones down now everyone. Please no more fighting,"

Claire took her place at the table and sighed at the sight of her cutlery set. She would have to buy a new one.

"I've never seen Poppy so glued to her phone," Mallory commented as Poppy was the last to put her phone away, "Who you texting?" she sang.

"It'll be Travis," Aaron declared through a mouthful of potato, "They're dating,"

"No we're not!"

Mallory gasped, "Poppy has a boyfriend?"

"We're just friends!"

"Sneaking off to see one another…" Aaron made kissing noises.

"Oh please, you do way more sneaking than I do!"

"Ah so you don't deny it!"

"I can assure you, every comment you make about me and Travis dating, it's a given that I'm denying it," Poppy jabbed her fork at her brother before stabbing it violently into a square of beef.

"We haven't heard from Travis in so long, you used to be good friends," Claire said, in an attempt to break the rising hostility.

"Yeah, we were,"

Claire sensed the tension in Poppy's tone, "How's his family?"

"I did a history report on them,"

Patrick coughed as he accidentally inhaled some of his food the wrong way, "You what?"

"Poppy, that's weird," Mallory snorted.

"No it's not!" sheargued, "I wrote a history report about his grandfather. He invented the Morris Mios and was murdered so Travis did some research with me about it because he was interested too,"

Nobody noticed Agatha twitch and turn to Poppy in recognition of the name.

"What kind of grandson has to research his grandfather's murder?" Patrick questioned.

"His mum doesn't talk to her mum," Poppy supplied, "They fell out or something,"

"That's strange," Claire said, "Edith was a lovely woman when I knew her, I don't understand why Harrison and Anna would cut her out like that,"

"You'd think she'd appreciate some support," Patrick added, "What with Anna's sister being the way she is,"

"Patrick," Claire said warningly.

"What's wrong with Anna's sister?" Aaron demanded, enjoying the sudden turn of conversation into gossip.

Claire sighed heavily, "She's not very well. She has little control over her mind. Unfortunately, at least this is what I've heard, it translates quite negatively through her… y'know,"

"Abilities?" Poppy finished derisively.

"Yes," Claire began vigorously slicing a piece of meat and refused to look at her daughter.

"She has a daughter too," Patrick continued, happily ignoring the glare from his wife, "Must be hard for her growing up with such an ill mother,"

"Travis has a cousin?"

"Yes, but I don't think this is a topic for our dinner table," Claire said firmly, "It is the Morris' lives and we should not be gossiping about them,"

"No one is going to know," Mallory shrugged, "Why was he murdered, Pop?"

"Because his invention was killing thousands of people and his brother wanted him to stop but he refused to,"

"His brother?!" Mallory gaped.

"Apparently!" Poppy interjected quickly, "There was no actual trial,"

"Why not?"

"Um, because he ran away,"

"Well that's a guilty man if I've ever heard one," Aaron laughed loudly.

"He probs did it Pops," Mallory confided to her.

"Yeah, probably," she agreed.

"Children please!" Claire asserted, "Not one more word about that family!"

"She's a bad woman that one," Agatha contributed throatily.

The whole family paused over their nearly empty plates and stared at the matriarch of the family. Agatha managed a spoonful of mashed potato before the lucid look in her eyes faded and they glazed once again.

"She said that when Travis was here," Poppy whispered.

"Who is she talking about?" Patrick also whispered, wary of breaking the fragile nature of the conversation. It was possible Agatha may say something else.

"Either his mum or grandma," Poppy responded, "But we're not sure which,"

Aaron leaned over the table, unwittingly dipping a hoodie drawstring into the gravy, and whispered theatrically across the table, "Ask Travis!"

"Travis doesn't know, that's the whole point!" Poppy's voice rose in infuriation, but she was smiling.

"You haven't been listening," Patrick smacked his son's shoulder with a fatherly slap.

Agatha was smiling too, settled once again in her family's familiar voices.

Claire rolled her eyes and began clearing the table, "Do not repeat any of this to Travis Poppy, nor you Aaron," she said as she stacked empty plates, "He might not know about his aunt or his cousin and it's not our place to tell him,"

The Dunkeany's scattered from the table. Mallory washed up as Patrick helped his mother into her armchair and then collected his papers from the kitchen floor, settling himself in the living room with Agatha to read through them again. Aaron and Poppy disappeared to their respective bedrooms after a final whispered conversation about Travis' family.

"Why do you think his mum refuses to talk to his

grandmother?" he asked.

Poppy shrugged.

"Which do you think is the bad one that Gran keeps talking about?"

She shrugged again, "I don't know Aaron, I just feel sorry for Travis having to put up with that kind of family drama,"

Later that evening, Poppy was lounging on her bed watching the tips of the pine trees bend slightly in the evening breeze, illuminated by the orange glow of the streetlamps. Various potted plants framed the window as well as lining the top of her desk, chest of drawers and her bookshelf. She held a book in her hands, opened on a page that had not been turned in the last ten minutes. She was thinking of Travis and worrying about what her feelings could mean.

She was happy. Happy with where their relationship was right now. She enjoyed spending time with him, they understood each other well, that was all. He listened to her, seemed genuinely interested in what she had to say, and he was funny too. But that didn't mean she wanted to date him. Aaron's words were running amok in her mind, planting seeds of doubt and thoughts that had not occurred to her before.

She frustratedly climbed to her feet, flinging the book aside. She had only been speaking to him again for a week! It hardly garnered such intense thinking. She grabbed her spray bottle and angrily misted her orchid that took pride of place on her bookshelf. For all she knew, Travis could drift away again like he did all those years ago. Many people struggled to feel comfortable around her, to accept her because of her stupid lack of ability. Not having a power meant some people were unable to gauge her personality or who she was.

Her father, Patrick, was a man of patience but strong, and this was reflected in his ability to manipulate and attract metal. He worked long hours at a recycling factory, gathering metal materials from the rest of the rubbish that could be melted down and re-used.

Claire's mothering and down to earth nature could be matched to her natural green thumb and ability to grow anything. She was gifted with the ability to determine which nutrient a plant was lacking or the reason behind its sudden wilting.

Mallory's ability to manipulate electrons demonstrated her impulsiveness and short-temper that was sometimes explosive. But she was also intelligent, spontaneous and had a magnetic personality. Aaron, on the other hand, was able to control any form of vibration. He mostly engaged it for pranks, by moving objects just out of reach or tripping unsuspecting victims up. Poppy even knew him to pressure her temples when he was really angry. But she also remembered him creating soft vibrations to help her sleep or to let a deaf person feel music.

Without an ability, Poppy was a blank slate. Enquiring after someone's ability was as common as asking their birthday or what their favourite hobby was. But who was Poppy? There was no power to define her. Once people discovered that, they either pitied her or feared her. There was so much of herself she could be hiding from them.

Perhaps Travis would be the same, she worried, tending to her plants on the windowsill. She repeatedly tried her 'growing thoughts', but they were overtaken by the idea that Travis could fear her and everything that was unknown about her. She realised that was why she talked so much about herself, to get everything out in the open so that nothing was hidden.

She sighed, her thoughts overtaken with anxiety and sadness. The plants seemed to wilt with her mood. How long before he faded away again?

Her phone vibrated on the windowsill, interrupting her contemplations. It was a message from Travis, asking if she was free to meet up on Saturday. She let the warmth fill her body. Yes, he may fade away again, but right now he was here, and she should enjoy it whilst she could.

Standing at the window, she noticed a faint movement through the glass. Curiosity overwhelmed her as she shaded her eyes and peered through. It was a figure. A figure who had just left their front garden, the gate swinging in their wake.

Poppy knew who that was.

She quickly pulled on her trainers and grabbed a jumper from the pile of discarded clothes on her chair and left the room. The plants on her windowsill watched as she careened down the front path and charged through the gate. They felt her mood and brightened, their leaves perking.

She was running, her trainers slapping on the pavement as she was alternatingly illuminated in an orange glow and then plunged into darkness. The figure was walking quickly, and she struggled to keep up.

As she rounded a corner, the figure had vanished. Poppy slowed to a jog but kept moving forwards. Suddenly the concrete beneath her violently erupted in a wave. It pushed upwards and she lost her balance, falling and scuffing her hands and knees.

"Oh God Pop! Are you okay, I didn't realise it was you!" Aaron pulled the hood back from his face as he appeared beside her and helped her to her feet.

"I'm good, don't worry!" she reassured him, "Where are you going Aaron? It's so late,"

"I'm only going out for a few hours, I'll be back in a bit,"

"But where?"

"I can't tell you,"

"Why not?" she demanded, "You tell me everything!"

"I can't tell you this time," he held firm, but there was an awkward, apologetic look entering his eyes.

"Can I come with you?"

He shook his head.

"But why? Are you in danger?"

"No nothing like that,"

"But-"

"You have to trust me,"

"But how can I do that when you won't even tell me where you're going? Or let me come with you?"

"Because you won't be able to do anything!" he snapped. The air felt electrified with the sudden vibrations that surrounded them, but they suddenly faded.

"Oh," her voice was quiet. She felt her bottom lip tremble.

Sometimes, when adolescents grew into their powers, they were curious to see how far they could push it, to reach their limit. Underground fights were popular as teenagers explored their powers as far as they could.

She had never been invited to one.

She understood why she was not welcome.

Powerless.

She roughly reminded herself she was not supposed to care about things like this.

The pair stood frozen, basking in the glow of the lamplight that turned their skins a sickly orange colour. Poppy was assaulted with a vision of the orange elephant treading towards her and all the trouble that followed it.

"Poppy, I-"

"No Aaron, I get it," she stepped back, away from her brother and out of the circle of light, "I'll just go home,"

CHAPTER 6
12th October 2019

The morning dawned cloudless and clear. The sun still held some warmth as Travis lifted his face towards it. The sky was a bottomless blue, the trees were a riot of colour like an autumnal blaze lining Poppy's street. Occasionally a tree would generously deliver a bright, burning leaf to his feet.

The air was quiet, and the slam of Poppy's front door echoed down the street. She waved cheerfully, a scarf wrapped around her neck and a knitted hat pulled low. He could not prevent a smile in response to her infectious grin.

"Maisie's again?" he asked.

"Can we go for a walk?" she stretched lethargically, "I prefer being outside,"

"Enjoy your date!" A voice called from an upstairs window. Travis caught Aaron's smirking face just before it vanished behind a closed curtain. So much for keeping this on the down low.

Poppy's light expression suddenly turned stormy and her eyes flashed from beneath the brim of her hat. She gripped Travis' elbow and proceeded to drag him away from her house.

"I am so angry with him," she steamed.

"How come?" Travis was barely able to match the speed of her furious march.

"He keeps disappearing," she finally let go of his elbow as she flicked her hands up in exasperation, "Going places late in the evening that he won't tell me. And he tells me everything,"

"Everything?" he repeated absentmindedly, he was still focused on the feeling her fingertips had left.

"Everything important," Poppy spared him a withering look before continuing, "I'm just so worried about him. You don't know where he's going, like where he was last night?"

"I'm sure he's fine," he reassured her, dodging the question. Of course, Travis knew that last night Aaron had nearly been crushed by an abandoned long-distance haulage trailer at the disused train tracks. He chose not to divulge this piece of information to Poppy.

"You think so?" she looked at him searchingly, seeking comfort.

He awkwardly nodded, his jaw clenching uncomfortably at lying to her.

"So," he cleared his throat, "Where do you want to go for a walk?"

Poppy's worried demeanour immediately brightened, "Westgate!" she announced, "I love the colour of the trees in autumn," she sighed wistfully, "And the best place to find trees is in a forest!"

He found himself unable to argue, despite the shift of guilt at the mention of Westgate. Allowing himself to be swept along in Poppy's cheer of the morning, the uncomfortable feeling dissipated. Even the relentless firing of questions in Travis' direction regarding his grandfather's death and family diatribes didn't particularly ruin it. She was just bad at hiding her morbid fascination.

"Yes, my Aunt Margaret isn't well," he confirmed at Poppy's direction, "But I don't know why either. My mum doesn't talk about her often,"

"What about her daughter?"

"My cousin?" Travis laughed, "She's so weird! She's called Bella or Bee, it's short for Arabella, right? So, I recently saw her a few months ago. She showed up on our doorstep and my mum was like 'I can't turn this girl away, she's got nothing to do with family arguments, so she invited her in," he began chuckling at the memory. She listened, entranced.

"So, she makes Bella a cup of tea and we sit with her and she just doesn't say anything!"

"That's, uh, odd?"

"Right?" he was laughing quite openly, "She honestly just sat there and stared at us as my mum talked at her. We asked after her mum obviously and she said she isn't well, but they don't really speak because she's bed bound,"

"She doesn't speak to her own mother?" Poppy repeated, horrified. She could not imagine not talking to her own mother, especially if she was so ill.

"They live in the same house and don't talk," Travis shook his head in disbelief, "She's an odd one. There's something not right about her. She's really, like, stuck up?"

"Aloof?" Poppy suggested.

"Exactly! She just stared at me as if she couldn't believe I was real. I think we were close once, but that was when I was really little. I think we had fun? I don't really remember her," he suddenly frowned, "Bella or Bee?" he muttered to himself, "There was two…?"

He shook his head, dislodging the pip of confusion, "What about your family? Your Nan sounded Irish?"

"Yeah, she left Ireland when she was sixteen because her Dad died, and she was pregnant. She used to tell us this story about how a mermaid got her pregnant," Poppy laughed at the sheer absurdity of the tale, "Dad says she tells it because she doesn't want to admit she had him out of wedlock,"

The pair had finally reached the edges of the sprawling forest that was Westgate. The forest was large, encompassing much of the northern side of the town, separating them from the intense weather produced by the mountains. She inhaled the sweet but smoky scent of the wilderness and exhaled contentedly.

"This is my favourite thing ever," she smiled, "I love all things green,"

"It's not looking that green right now," Travis commented, observing the browning of the leaves and collection of mud and mulch on the forest floor. They crunched under their feet as they entered the shelter of the canopy.

"Can you change the colour of living things?" Poppy enquired. He noticed her examining his expression, as if waiting on a particular answer.

"Sort of,"

She continued watching him sceptically, "Example?"

The memory arrived completely unwarranted in his mind. The elephant whose trunk he had managed to turn orange when they were both eight years old.

"Oh, I don't know," he said, faking nonchalance, "Maybe an elephant?"

"You do remember the orange elephant!" she stared at him, aghast.

"Yeah, 'course,"

"Do you have any idea how much trouble I got in for that?" she stared at him in disbelief, "I drew it in class and got into trouble because elephants aren't orange!"

"Seriously?"

"Yeah, the teacher brought it up at my parents' evening. I had to discuss my 'disconnection from reality' in a therapy session a few months later,"

"You had a therapist?" he asked, still reeling from the fact that his prank had caused such discord.

"Well technically no, he wasn't a therapist, more of like a guidance counsellor," she waved her hand dismissively, "But he wasn't very good. Made it out that it was all my fault,"

Travis scrunched his nose up in a frown, "How's it your fault?"

"Well that's the thing, I don't think it is," Poppy plucked a late blooming flower from the ground and placed it in her hair, "It's not like I actively sat there as a child and decided 'I'm not going to have any abilities,"

"But that's what he implied," he finished for her.

"That's what he implied," she agreed.

They walked for a little longer, enjoying the sheltered silence of the forest. After steadily climbing, they reached the edge of a slope that tumbled away before them to the River Magnus on the eastern side of the forest. There was a fallen tree, its trunk lying at the perfect angle to create a bench for the two of them.

Poppy hopped up without hesitation, settling herself securely and easily on the rough bark. Travis hauled himself up beside her, straddling the trunk uncomfortably as he struggled to balance.

"Isn't it beautiful?" she stretched her arms wide as if embracing the scenery.

"Sure is," he winced, shifting his weight.

They fell into silence and Travis watched as Poppy closed her eyes and let the filtered sunlight fall on her face. He thought she was beautiful. For a brief moment, he saw her as she would be in several years' time. He wondered what she would be doing. He hoped she would still be hauling him out for walks to hug the landscape.

"What do you want to do when you're older?" his voice had posed the question before he realised.

She turned to him, her hair erupting in waves from her hat down past her shoulders. Her russet brown eyes caught the light in flecks of gold as she thoughtfully considered the question.

"I want to help people like me," she pulled her knees up to her chest and rested her chin on them, staring wistfully off into some distant future, "I realise that not everyone like me is like me," She screwed her face up in derision at her own words, "If you get what I mean?"

He nodded, entranced by the way her face lit up when she spoke of something she was passionate about.

"There are other children out there who will be powerless, and it will be the worst thing ever for them. They will be so angry and disappointed, and I don't want them ending up with someone like my counsellor who implies that it's their fault. I've pretty much accepted that it's the hand I've been dealt, but I doubt that's the case for everyone in this situation. And there are some that demand that everyone else hides their abilities in public spaces to protect the feelings of those few,"

"Oh yeah, I've heard of them," Travis struggled to hide the contempt in his voice.

"Exactly!" she grinned, "That's the exact response of everyone! Because it is a totally unfair request to make. We need to teach the powerless that they are no less than everyone around them because they're not the same, but we can't do that at the expense of the rest,"

"You've really thought about this, haven't you?"

"It was all I ever thought about when I first found out," she admitted, "I had to learn really quickly how to handle people's responses. And then my own feelings to those responses, and how I wanted to feel. I feel like a control freak sometimes, that has to constantly monitor and reflect on their feelings,"

She let out a frustrated sigh, "I'm not making much sense, am I?"

He shook his head frantically, "Yes, yes you are!" he responded passionately, "It's totally reasonable to want to control yourself after being so, y'know, powerless,"

Her gaze drifted again to the distant mountains, "Accurate. What about you?"

He shrugged, "I haven't really thought about it, there's not a lot I can do. Not like my powers are really that helpful," he thought for a moment, "Maybe something to do with animals,"

"Oh, like elephants?" Poppy suggested playfully.

"Aaron was saying last night about-" Travis began and stopped, tensing as he realised he had given himself away to her.

She turned her head slowly to face him as she came to terms with what he said, "Last night?" she murmured quietly. She pinned him with an accusatory glare, "You said you weren't with him last night?"

Travis froze, his mind racing, "I mean, technically I didn't say-"

"You were with him," Poppy interrupted, "What's he doing Travis? I've heard all sorts of things about those fake Chikara fights! You have to tell me where they're happening!"

"Fights?" he responded, bemused, "We're not involved in any Chikara fights,"

Yet, he added internally.

Cogs whirring, she chewed the inside of her cheek. If Aaron was not getting into fights, what was he doing? She knew it had something to do with abilities, because why else would he have been so against her coming with him last night?

"Isn't he sneaking off to Chikara fights?"

"Absolutely not," his gaze slid over the surrounding trees, avoiding eye contact with Poppy in case she could tell that he was lying. The four of them were not sneaking off to Chikara fights, but what they were doing wasn't much better. His gaze found something far more distracting, however. The strange man was there again. Travis felt his muscles contract in a fight or flight response.

"Travis?" Poppy hissed. She was talking but he couldn't hear what she was saying over the pounding of the blood in his temples. His heart rocketed around his ribcage, acid building in his throat. The man was standing about a hundred yards away behind them, partially hidden by the bare branches of blackberry bushes.

"Poppy?" he managed in a strangled whisper.

"What?" she had folded her arms and was pouting at him.

He tore his eyes from the man and fixed them on Poppy's. The connection allowed him to catch his breath enough for his heart to stop racing so wildly.

"Do you see that man?" he muttered, gesturing subtly with a nod of his head.

She frowned in brief confusion, thrown by the sudden change in subject. She glanced towards where Travis had indicated, and saw her eyes widen in shock at the sight of the dishevelled man. They latched back onto his and her lip quivered as she demanded, "Why's he there?"

"Um, so, he's been following me for a few days now,"

"He's been what?!" her voice rose an octave in disbelief, "You have to confront him!"

"Are you crazy?" he whispered furiously back, "We don't know what he can do! And we're a bit useless ourselves. I can only change colours and you can't do anything!"

Her face turned stony and she looked away, ashamed. Travis felt a lump lodge steadfastly in his throat. How could he take that back?

"Poppy, you know I didn't mean-"

"I can do something," she jutted her chin defiantly as she glared at him, "I can confront him,"

Before he could stop her, she had leapt from her perch on the log and was hurtling forwards into the undergrowth.

"Hey!" she waved her arms manically, "Hey, I'm talking to you!"

The stranger stumbled backwards hurriedly. He seemed frightened to have finally been approached. He started to move away, seeking cover amongst the trees.

"What do you want?" she shouted at the retreating figure, "Wait! Don't run! Stay where you are!" She forged ahead in response, crunching dried grass and fallen leaves beneath her boots.

The figure stumbled and appeared to fall over his own

feet. Both Travis and Poppy were too far away to see the wrinkled roots creep up from the forest ground and encircle the stranger's feet. The stranger fell and cursed and desperately tried to detangle his feet from the vines as Poppy marched relentlessly towards him. With shaking hands, he desperately pulled and ripped at the vines to free his ankles but to no avail.

Poppy was almost upon the stranger. She could see the ripped coat, the fingerless gloves, the dirtied beanie. She saw the edges of a tangled beard and realised she was approaching an aged man who was also as much a stranger to a shower as he was to her.

Suddenly flamers were flickering around the man's feet. Poppy halted, stumbled back several steps as the flames briefly caught some of the scattered leaves on the forest's floor. Within seconds of the flames igniting, the man had launched to his feet and was running. He spryly dodged between trees, leaping madly. Poppy likened his movement to that of a scared swimmer in a seaweed-laden ocean. He was wildly hitching his knees up as if something were grabbing at his ankles.

She watched him run, her head tilted in deliberation at the vanishing spectre that was still smoking around the cuffs of his trousers. Travis skidded to a stop beside her, breathing heavily.

"You're crazy!" was all he could say.

"You've seen that man how many times and you haven't thought to actually try to speak to him?" she asked.

"He would've just run away though," Travis argued pathetically. He did not want to admit to Poppy that the man scared him. He was frightened by the feeling of familiarity that the stranger's face elicited in him.

"Who do you think he is?"

He could tell her, he thought. He could tell her that he had a vague recollection of the stranger's face. The familiar eyes, nose, expression. It had taken him several days to match the man to the photograph that stood proudly on his mother's dressing table. The stranger following him was a ruffled and aged version of his murdered grandfather.

CHAPTER 7
16th July 2011

Ellen Davies was panicking.

She desperately counted the sea of excitable heads before her again. Twenty-seven. Twenty-eight. No, that wasn't right. There should be thirty.

"Children please, stay still!" she called, harried to the point her hands were shaking. She managed to disguise the anxiety in her voice, "I need to do a head count,"

The sea of seven and eight-year-olds obediently stilled to a soft current of movement, unable to stop moving completely. One child let out an uncontainable woop as he created a sudden breeze that knocked all hats from heads. Ellen suppressed the power without thinking, grunting with frustration as little bodies suddenly dropped and scrambled around on the ground.

Once again, she only counted twenty-eight. She still had two missing children. She had become distracted again, thinking of that handsome gentleman from the night before. He was a doctor, specialising in the psychology of children who failed to develop an ability. Such a noble cause to help those poor little things…

She snapped back to reality. Who on earth had thought a

trip of thirty school children to the local zoo had been a good idea? These children were hard enough to keep track of in the classroom, never mind in a maze of attractions filled with a myriad of exotic animals.

Ellen subtly waved a teaching assistant over (God forbid she accidentally beckoned a parent helper over) and issued him with a stark warning, "We must find these children immediately, otherwise we will have hell to pay!" The poor assistant nodded and hurried away towards the tigers and lions, a stark image of torn children's clothing and carnivorous cats licking their lips filling his mind.

The two children in question, Poppy Dunkeany and Travis Lee, were in fact located in the opposite direction by the elephant enclosure. They were locked in an intense discussion regarding Travis' newly discovered abilities.

"I don't believe you!" Poppy was shouting and stamping her foot in an effort to demonstrate to Travis how much she didn't believe him.

"It's true!" he pouted in response, "I can change the colour of anything! I have lots of… of…" he paused as he tried to remember the word, "Biochromes!" he blurted at last.

Poppy gasped, "They're not a real thing!"

He tugged at the hem of his t-shirt, his face glowing with embarrassment and anger, "They are too!" he whined.

"You have to prove it," she demanded stubbornly, "You have to change the colour of something,"

He straightened and puffed his chest at the challenge, "I'll turn that elephant orange!" he announced.

Poppy looked over at the great but gentle quadruped. It was swinging its trunk, occasionally stretching upwards as if to catch the afternoon sunlight. She nodded at it, content with Travis' choice.

He suddenly looked nervous, "'Though I don't know how to get it over here," he mumbled, "I'm not backing out or anything!" he assured quickly, "I just don't wanna go in there,"

"That's okay," Poppy responded, clambering partially up

the fence and leaning over it, "She'll come to us,"

The elephant's lumbering head swung towards the two children and the thickly lashed eyes settled on Poppy. It sloped slowly towards the two of them, reluctantly placing its large cylindrical feet in the sand. It was as if it had heard her yearning and some invisible force was drawing it near.

"You can prove it now," she said matter-of-factly, as the elephant extended its trunk lethargically over the fence. She reached upwards and felt the trunk tremble as her fingertips touched it. The elephant sighed and wavered, relaxing to her touch.

Travis screwed up his face in concentration, his tongue stubbornly sticking out. He reached up, touching the elephant and straining.

Poppy watched in awe as the elephant's wrinkled skin began to flicker and pulse, the colour orange spreading like the redness blushing Travis' cheeks.

"It's working! It's working!" she squealed excitedly.

It was as the orange was spreading over the forehead of the elephant that Travis suddenly gasped for air and collapsed to his knees.

Poppy dropped quickly, kneeling at his side as she stared deeply at him, "Too much?"

He nodded, "Too much,"

The elephant shook its head, its ears flapping, and trod slowly away. It was uncertain as to what had just happened. A tickling in its trunk and its eyes. The gentle caress of the young girl. It had no idea it had just turned orange. Elephants are colour blind.

22nd July 2011

Poppy steadfastly refused to speak to her parents during the journey to Dr Thackery. Her school had broken up a few days before, yet she had been denied her endless days of summer fun by these counselling sessions. She stubbornly kicked her feet against the plastic chairs in the waiting room, snubbed the gentleman at the reception desk, and maintained a dour expression.

She was too young to understand the implications of having no abilities. She was under the impression that they would still eventually come to her.

"Poppy Dunkeany?" a tall man, with thick framed glasses and a tie called her name. He wore a classic white doctor's coat, and it frightened her. Her parents gently pushed her forward, and she reluctantly allowed herself to be led into the room.

The man introduced himself as Dr Clarence Thackery, a recent mature graduate who had gained a doctorate in the subject of children's ability development.

"I wouldn't consider myself a therapist or psychologist," he explained to Claire and Patrick, "I haven't got that sort of training, but I am qualified in helping children who fail to display an ability. I help them to come to terms with living powerless, as well as how to interact with a world that will try to ostracise them,"

Poppy had seen an Ostrich at the zoo. She decided against enlightening Thackery with that information, he smelled too weird and she didn't like him very much.

"Okay Poppy, would you like to take a seat?" he gestured to a lone, wood chair opposite a large armchair. It had been painted in primary colours in an attempt to make it more inviting.

She looked to her parents for support, but they had settled themselves on a sofa in the corner, awkwardly squeezed together. She cautiously sat in the chair. It was very uncomfortable.

"Okay Poppy, my name is Dr Thackery. I want to just have a chat with you about some issues your teacher has raised, okay?"

She sat still, unwilling to commit to the conversation.

"So we're going to do a few tests to see if you have any kind of ability, but first, I want to talk to you about the orange elephant,"

A shadow passed over her face. Miss Davies had shouted a lot about the drawing of Poppy's orange elephant. She still didn't understand why.

"Where did you see it?"

"At the zoo," she said quietly.

"Are you sure it was orange?"

"Yes!" Poppy felt tears well up in her eyes even though she felt angry. Why did no one believe her? Why couldn't Travis come here and admit he had done it?

"The issue here, Poppy, is that this is what we call a disconnection from reality. It's something that we need to work on before we can start talking about your abilities,"

She stared blankly.

"Do you think you have abilities Poppy?"

She shook her head.

"That's good," Thackery nodded encouragingly, "That's what we call acceptance,"

"I figured I just haven't got them yet," she added, "I just need to keep trying and practicing,"

"And that's what we call denial," Patrick whispered to Claire.

Sitting motionlessly, his hands paused in their notetaking, Thackery said gently, "I think it's best if you stop trying now Poppy,"

Unable to comprehend why this man was telling her to stop searching for her powers, Poppy floundered. She felt a sinking in her chest, a feeling that would become all too familiar as she is repeatedly told during that Summer that her powers would not come to her.

Sensing her bewilderment, Thackery changed tact, "Orange elephants aren't real," he said kindly, but Poppy could hear a firm edge to his voice now, similar to how her mother's voice hardened just before she began scolding, "They wouldn't survive very well in the wild if they were, would they?"

"Why not?"

"They'd be easier for predators to see Poppy, they'd be a great orange beacon,"

She frowned. At the zoo, the sign had said elephants had no natural predators because they were so big. She weighed her options. She could continue arguing, but with no proof it was becoming a pointless endeavour. She realised that she would spend the whole summer having this conversation on a loop. She didn't like the way he was making her feel. Maybe if she agreed, she could go early?

She conceded defeat, "Orange elephants aren't real,"

CHAPTER 8
16th October 2019

Poppy and Aaron were lying on the sofa watching trash TV when Mallory thundered into the house. Aaron was stretched out, still wearing a crumpled school shirt, with his feet on the coffee table. Poppy was buried to her chin beneath a fleecy blanket. Both faces held the glazed, zombified look of those who had spent far too long staring at a TV screen.

"Why is she crying?" even Agatha had a similar look; her knitting lying unnoticed in her lap.

"She's just got divorced," Poppy explained, "But her husband has done it behind her back,"

Agatha developed a look of deep sorrow, "How awful,"

"It gets worse Gran," Aaron added gleefully, "He told her by text!"

Agatha tutted and sighed.

Mallory marched in front of the television screen, blocking its distracting power. Poppy and Aaron's faces contorted briefly into rage and disbelief before Mallory held her hands up and announced, "I have gossip,"

"What gossip?" An intrigued expression stole across

Poppy's face as her brother dramatically threw his arms up and rolled his eyes.

"What's so important it's interrupting my trash TV time?" he demanded.

"I'm amazed you're not watching Chikara fights right now,"

"Just spit it out,"

"You'll never guess who I heard Naomi talking to,"

They both blinked blankly at her, devoid of ideas.

"Travis's Nan,"

"What!" Poppy gaped, "Why?"

Aaron was a bit more sceptical, "How do you know it was her? Did you see her?"

"Well, no, but-"

"Then how do you know?"

"Well, Naomi called her Ms Morris,"

"How do you know there aren't loads of Ms Morrises?" Aaron countered, "She has two daughters, remember?"

"Yeah, but one is married with the surname Lee and the second one is Miss," Poppy interjected, "It must have been her, but why?"

Mallory smirked at her brother, "She said her brother-in-law was back and she needed to find him," she added.

"Brother-in-law as in Joseph Morris as in murderer?" Poppy asked tentatively, her voice barely above a whisper. The man they had seen in the woods, the one who had been following Travis, could it have been Joseph? A murderous great uncle?

Aaron sensed her sudden uneasiness, detecting the stiffness in her posture, "You okay?"

"Were there any other brothers?" Mallory queried.

Poppy shook her head. She knew the family tree weirdly well now, having written about it in her history report. Her stomach roiled at the possibility that she had willingly run towards a murderer in the woods.

"Then yeah, murderer. Speaking of which-" Mallory began, but Poppy interrupted her.

"We've seen him!" she blurted, "Travis has seen him multiple times! And I saw him when we went for a walk in Westgate,"

"You went for a walk in Westgate? Why?" Aaron sat up, pulling his feet off the table. Tension sat heavily on his shoulders. His toe began to tap rhythmically, his bouncing knee.

"I wanted to see the views, they're so nice on a clear day," Poppy explained defensively. She noticed her brother visibly relax as he learnt where in the woods she had been, "What's wrong with me being in Westgate?"

"There's nothing wrong with it," Aaron sighed, collapsing back into the sofa cushions.

"I think the more important question, Aaron, is what do you mean you've seen him?" Mallory shouted exasperatedly, her voice catching in her throat. She tugged distractedly at her braids. "There's everything wrong with being in Westgate when there's a murderer loose!"

"It might not have been him," Poppy suggested, attempting to pacify the situation. She was aware how immensely protective Mallory could become when she thought her younger siblings were in danger. She didn't want her to worry, nor enter the state where she would demand to know their whereabouts every hour. Poppy herself had also massively jumped conclusions. It might not have been Joseph at all.

"Explain exactly what happened," Mallory ordered.

She sighed, "We just saw a man in the woods and Travis said it was a bloke who seemed to be following him. I shouted at the man, but he ran off before I could get to him. He fell over and I nearly got there, but he must have, like, a fire ability of some sort because he tried to scare me off with flames,"

Mallory was silent. She touched her forehead with her fingertips, her face worryingly unreadable. Both Poppy and Aaron tensed as the living room lights flickered, waiting for the explosion.

"He scared you off with flames," Mallory repeated through gritted teeth.

"It could have been anyone!" Poppy protested.

"So what?!" Mallory yelled, her voice trembling, "So what it could have been anyone! You were still in danger Poppy!"

"Hardly!"

"No, that's it," Mallory clapped, signalling she had come to a decision. Agatha had been sitting tensely, listening to the children argue, but the harsh sound caused her to jump. The ornaments on the mantle piece rattled, but the glue held them in place.

"I'm telling Mum and Dad when they get home and we are going to enforce a family curfew,"

Aaron snorted in disgust, "Total snitch,"

"You can't tell anyone!" Poppy complained.

"I just want you safe!" Mallory responded, baffled, "Fine, I won't tell but I want you back before dark and that means you stay home. No sneaking out to whatever it is you do at night Aaron,"

"It gets dark at like six!" Aaron pushed himself to his feet infuriated, the air vibrating menacingly around him as he stormed from the room, "Seriously Mal, it's totally safe,"

"I couldn't be more serious right now, both of you," Mallory glared at Poppy, ignoring Aaron as he walked away, "That man is really dangerous. You've just said he can create flames from nothing. He could be a wanted murderer for God's sake! This man could really hurt you,"

CHAPTER 9
16th October 2019

Travis entered his kitchen to find the stranger who had been following him sitting at the breakfast table, nursing a mug of tea.

He froze. His school bag, gripped in his right hand, began undulating wildly through the rainbow as he panicked. Questions rushed through his head as he tried to make sense of what he was seeing. Had he broken in? Broken in to make tea? How did he know where he lived?

The man's coat was discarded on the back of another chair, and the holes in his knitted jumper were obvious. The tangled edges of the forest green thread seemed singed and blackened. Travis noted raw red marks on the man's head, now free of its beanie. It was almost as if he had been burned, but what caused burns in the shape of hands?

As he began to slowly back out of the kitchen, he felt a hand suddenly fall on his shoulder. He yelled, flinging his arm out in a panic, catching his mother across the face.

"Travis!" Anna Lee scolded her son as she adjusted her spectacles, "What an earth is wrong with you?"

"Who the hell is he?" Travis hissed. They both looked to the man, who continued to sip from his tea and fiddle idly with the threads of his jumper's sleeve, completely unaware of their presence. Travis looked to his mother, "Have you put a wall up?"

Anna nodded. She pushed her spectacles up her nose, but the effort of maintaining her 'wall' – an invisible barrier that was able to block soundwaves - was causing her to sweat and they slid down again, "You haven't met this man before," she said through gritted teeth, "But he is my Uncle Joseph,"

Travis' chest suddenly tightened, and he was overwhelmed with a wave of cold fear, "Didn't he kill his brother?" his voice emerged as a whisper.

The soundproof wall suddenly dropped and the man, Joseph Morris, flinched at the sound of Anna's hand connecting with the back of her son's head, "Where the hell did you hear that?" she demanded.

"Have you ever read an article about our family?" Travis responded, angrily rubbing the sore spot on the back of his head, "That's all they say, along with how Grandad single-handedly killed thousands of people," he added sarcastically.

A gasp pulled Anna and Travis from their argument. Joseph was leaning heavily over the table, silently convulsing.

"Oh Jay, I didn't mean for you to hear that," Anna rushed forward, but her sudden movement panicked Joseph. He lurched to his feet, his arms jutting out erratically as he pushed himself away from the table. The chair clattered to the ground behind him. He rushed to the back door, his wrist careening wildly into the mug, sending a cascade of tea over the edge of the table.

Anna rushed after him as he escaped into the garden. Travis was left alone in the silence, stunned by the sudden animalistic panic displayed by his great uncle. A drop of tea occasionally detached itself from the pool on the tabletop, committing to the long fall and final splash as it connected with the linoleum. Travis hastily threw a tea towel over the mess, picking up the now cracked mug. Muffled voices drew him to the kitchen window, and he watched uneasily as Joseph clumsily crouched and clutched at his head.

Travis watched his mother clutch at Joseph's wrists, speaking desperately, trying to pull his hands away from his scalp. Then Travis saw the smoke. Joseph was burning himself in his panic. His fingertips glowed stronger and stronger, and Anna seemed unable to bring him back from wherever his mind at gone.

Travis clutched at the mug. It undulated threw dim, murky colours. He groped through
his mind, searching for some way that he could help, but his mind had stalled, frozen like his body. Eventually, Joseph settled, no longer scrabbling and scratching at his head. He grew still, holding Anna's hands, slumped in on himself.

When they both clambered to their feet, Travis stumbled away from the window and began rubbing the teacloth around the table in a vain attempt to wipe away the tea that had already sunk into the wood.

"I need you to treat Jay's burns, okay?" Anna quietly said to him as she led Joseph back into the kitchen, "They're just around his hairline,"

"How do I do that? I've never treated burns before," Travis felt fear bloom in his chest. Joseph was a mystery to him, one that was prone to sudden bouts of frenzied self-destructive panic. What would happen when Travis touched him? Would he bolt again? Or would he burn him?

"Well it's time you learnt," Anna responded gently, "I need to sort my own burns okay," she showed him the reddened skin on her palms and the edge of her index fingers, "I'll be right back with the first aid kit. Run some cool water, not cold, and soak two tea towels,"

She left the room, Travis staring dumbly after her, and with that he was left alone with Joseph. Joseph was absent-mindedly rubbing his palms together anxiously. Along his hairline were bright, ugly pink finger marks that were beginning to swell.

Before he could stop himself, Travis blurted, "Are you okay?"

Joseph stared at him. His pale, blue eyes were piercing.

"Yes," he finally said gruffly through his beard.

Travis nodded and began running cool water, soaking cloths with it to make compresses. His mother returned, directing him to hold a compress over his great uncle's burns. So, Travis found himself pressing two tea towels to his uncle's temples and intermittently apologising for the cold water that was dribbling down either side of the old man's face.

"So, this is Travis," Anna introduced as she ran her hands under cool water, "He's my son. And Travis, this my Uncle Jay, or Joseph,"

"Hi there," Travis tried, feeling the time for introductions had already passed. He had already seen Joseph have a breakdown and was now holding his head between two soaked tea towels like a soggy, unappetising sandwich.

Joseph only grunted.

"I remember all the time we spent together," Anna pushed forward regardless, "You, me, Dad and Margaret,"

Joseph's face remained stony. Travis watched as he receded deeper into himself at the mention of his family.

The room descended into an uncomfortable silence. Eventually, Anna broke it with a frustrated sigh, "Where have you been all this time?" she demanded, "Arriving on my doorstep after 40 years. I didn't even recognise you," she admonished.

Joseph stubbornly remained quiet. Travis could sense a muscle ticking in his great uncle's jaw, but he focused on controlling his stress and not unintentionally changing the colour of Joseph's head.

Anna threw her cloth on the table and stormed from the room. Her footsteps abruptly stopped, and Travis knew she had put a wall in place, probably so she could scream her frustration in peace.

"Uh, do you-"

Joseph swivelled suddenly in his chair, his chin jutting defiantly, "I didn't do it, no matter what the papers or anyone says,"

Travis averted his eyes from the intense gaze, "Yeah, sure, I believe you," he said.

Joseph followed him searchingly as Travis threw the cloths in the sink and rummaged for aloe vera cream in the first aid kit.

"Seems like you don't," Joseph said sceptically.

"Then why did you run?" Travis demanded, "Why are you here? Y'know I've read every newspaper and history article on this family. They've written loads on us, and made countless TV shows and documentaries," the words were pouring out in an unstoppable wave. The pent up frustration and rage and confusion he felt, ever since researching his family with Poppy, came flooding out.

"And it is so messed up. I actually don't blame Mum for deliberately keeping me in the dark about it," the bottle of cream clutched in his hand had turned an ugly red, "But I've seen more of my grandmother in interviews than I have in real life because of this,"

Joseph rhythmically began knocking on the wood, counting under his breath. Travis sensed he had gone too far; he had released his pent-up anger on the wrong person. He braced, expecting another eruption.

Instead, Joseph held a trembling hand out, "I'll put my own cream on, I don't need you massaging my temples,"

Travis gave him the bottle with no resistance.

"So, what's your ability?" Joseph asked, disconcerted by the sudden change in colour of the bottle as it passed hands.

"Chromatophoric Kinaesthetic," Travis recited.

"Eh?"

"I can manipulate melanophore packets in the chromatophores of Biochromes," he explained, "And I have an excess so can change the colour of inanimate objects,"

"So you change the colours of things?" Joseph confirmed, as he began gently rubbing the cream onto his burns.

"Only when I'm touching it,"

"Huh," Joseph seemed to chew the information over, "That's not what I thought it was,"

"How'd you mean?"

"Well, in the woods, I had vines wrapping round my feet,"

"Is that why you tripped?"

Joseph nodded.

"Wasn't me,"

"The girl?" Joseph suggested.

"No, she hasn't got any powers,"

"Oh,"

"And you can make fire, huh?"

Joseph gave a look of fake, dumb-founded surprise, "How did you guess?" he asked drily.

"Just my incredible intuition,"

They lapsed into silence briefly. Through the thin walls of the house, they could hear Anna angrily ordering a pizza over the phone.

"How is you Grandmother?" Joseph asked suddenly, "You said you saw more of her on TV?"

Travis shrugged, "We don't talk to her," He was conscious that Joseph had not answered any of his questions, like why he had left and why he had suddenly appeared again that week.

"What about Margaret?"

Travis shrugged again, "Mum talks to her sometimes, but I don't think she's doing too well,"

Joseph buried his face in his hands, "I shouldn't have left," he mumbled.

"Would it have made a difference? I mean-" Travis tried to justify his words as Joseph impaled him with a scowl, "If you had stayed you would have gone to prison anyways,"

"I could have done something," he growled.

Anna returned to the kitchen, announcing that she had ordered a pizza. She checked Joseph's burns and was pleased to see there were no blisters beginning to form, meaning they wouldn't need a trip to hospital and risk Joseph's discovery.

"Travis, can you go pick up the pizza?" Anna asked pointedly.

"What's the point in ordering if you don't order to the house?" Travis complained as Anna ushered him out of the kitchen and down the hallway.

"I need to try and talk to him," she hissed as she tugged a hat violently onto his head.

Travis, now slightly disorientated, struggled to pull a coat on as he said, "I'm out tonight anyways,"

Usually, this statement was followed by at least some form of interrogation, demands of where he was going or who he was with. The familiar tug of guilt at lying to his mother about his evening excursions, however, was abated this evening. If she was keeping secrets from him, there was nothing wrong with a little white lie of his own every now and again, was there?

Anna distractedly nodded and waved him out the door.

...

Later that evening when he returned home from another exhausting evening, Travis found his mother standing in the darkened doorway of their living room, watching Joseph sleep on their sofa. She was chewing the corner of a nail, a nervous habit. Orange lamp light from the street filtered through the glazed glass of the front door and bathed the hallway in an eerie glow.

Travis watched as Joseph's sleep was disturbed with nightmares, he rolled and kicked and mumbled in his sleep. She put an arm around him, "Good night?"

He ignored the question, quickly turning away as he felt like an intruder, "Why is he like that?" he whispered.

Anna sighed, and slowly closed the living room door, "He didn't do well in the war," her voice was so quiet, Travis almost didn't hear her, "I was too young to remember him leaving, but I remember him coming home when I was four. All I remember of him for those two years was a kind and loving man, but there was always something off about him. There was one incident, at the supermarket, the bin bags…" she trailed off. Her voice wobbled as she tried again, "It wasn't until my father…"

"You don't have to talk about this if you don't want to,"

"My father was killed, but not by him," her voice was firm, although her eyes shined wetly in the dark, "I don't know who did it, but it wasn't him. I lost every single member of my family after that,"

Travis failed to respond, unable to even comprehend the words he would need to say to comfort his mother. Luckily, she continued in hushed tones, "You can't tell anyone he's here, okay? Promise me,"

"Okay,"

"Say it,"

"I promise,"

ESSENCE

CHAPTER 10
20th October 2019

The grounds of the Morris estate began life as a marshland. Long before the railway tracks were built, or even combustion engines invented, the woods tumbled bemusedly into the boggy grounds of the marsh. Their roots intertwined with the tough grasses and the water-logged mud seeped between the wood, making them more prone to rot.

In these times, abilities were still heavily misunderstood.

Will-o'-the-wisps were common here, shepherding unwary travellers into trouble. They guided then tricked, seemingly led straight but curved in circles. Stories of these impish glows permeated legends. Many claimed them to be spirits, or goblins, or elves.

Here, in this desolate marshland, they belonged to a young, bored boy.

Starved of attention, with a father who was rarely home and a mother who was continually swept off her feet, the boy played with the lights he created. He began by rolling them between his fingertips, but when that grew repetitive, he rolled them back and forth across the floor. His mother quickly grew tired of tripping over her son, so sent him out with the flick of her broom.

The boy grew to like the way his pockets of lights would flicker in the afternoon haze. They would float haphazardly, lazily guided by his thoughts. He liked them especially at night, however. Their hypnotic glow soothed him, providing the illusion of beauty and grace amongst the ugly reeds.

Local townsfolk soon discovered the glowing orbs that only appeared at night. They would gather at the edge of the marsh like a swarm of flies to rotting meat. Pointing, gasping, whittering, they disturbed the boy's peace.

He found himself furious the first-time townsfolk reached out to touch his light. He tugged it away reflexively, violated, but a single, persistent man followed. He lurched into the marsh, desperate to feel the little orb. The boy pulled further and further away, and the man followed, wallowing and wading in the mud.

Until the boy led him to a deceptively firm patch of grass. The marsh swallowed the townsman greedily. The boy had guided the man to his death. The marsh belched its thanks.

The exciting whispers of the glowing orbs quickly transformed into terrified muttered warnings.

Do not stray to the marsh at night.

Ignore the little balls of light.

Beware of the will-o'-the-wisps, because they will lead you to your death.

It was late one evening, as the boy sat carelessly chewing a reed and gazing at the stars, that his father chose this night to return home. Leaving the town late, darkness fell unexpectedly quickly as clouds scudded uglily across the horizon. The father reached the edge of the marsh that lay spitefully between him and his home. By the day, the marsh was tricky crossing, by night a trap.

But what's this?

A small light bobbed brightly, brushing the tips of the

grasses. A Will-o'-the-wisp!

The father had heard of these. Despite the temptation, despite the inviting nature of the lights, one must ignore them! The boy watched in growing frustration, then anger and, finally, horror as his father steadfastly turned away from each light that tried to guide him to the safety of his home.

It was not long before the marsh claimed its honoured victim.

And so, the boy grew old. The boy died. The marshland grew old. The marshland dried. The forest blossomed at the expense of the marsh, able to spread eagerly and grow well. Eventually, settlers expanded away from the centre of town, and a wealthy family founded their home on the plot of the boy's drowned father.

The home of the Morris family nestled contentedly on the southern edge of Westgate Forest, ignorant to the skeletons that lay beneath its foundations. There had been direct links to the railway tracks, but the family had long since walled off their land. If one were to follow the track south, down the western edge of Westgate Woods, a great seven-foot-high brick wall would block the path.

Luckily, Poppy entered the grounds via the more convenient route: the front gates. She wiped strands of hair from her sweating forehead, tired from her march across town. She was still fuming at Mallory for abandoning her to face this alone, and thus making her walk the entire way.

She pulled her hat off as she approached the house, suddenly awe-struck by the glamorous façade. Leafy hedges and bushes bordered the veranda, still full and luscious despite the time of year. Poppy paused at several plants, sensing a contentedness in their poise. The front of the house was pleasingly symmetric, with crystal white window frames set comfortably into their brick casings.

She climbed the steps that featured a cascade of plant pots, and pulled at the great brass knocker, letting it fall with a reverberating bong noise.

Edith Morris eventually answered. She found Poppy crouched beside the smallest pot, admiring the colourful cosmos flowers. She coughed and Poppy leapt to her feet.

"Hello dear," she smiled, and Poppy winced slightly as her lips pulled tight, "I greatly appreciate you visiting to continue our discussion from the other day,"

"That's okay," Poppy tried to return the smile, but it seemed to get stuck halfway, "You have a very pretty garden,"

"Oh, do you garden?" Edith asked politely as she ushered Poppy inside and shut the front door. The hallway was dim, but Edith's expensive but garish, fuchsia pink cashmere cardigan glowed in the gloom. Her hair had been professionally coloured, but it could not hide the fact that it was beginning to thin on her scalp.

"Yes," Poppy removed her coat and folded it neatly over one arm, "I do it a lot with my Mum,"

"Oh, I get someone in to do it," Edith waved a hand dismissively and sauntered further into the house.

Poppy made to follow, but was blocked by a girl standing in the centre of the hallway, her gaze fixated on a glass cabinet. Her hair, so fair it was almost white, hung lankly, clinging closely to her skull so that she appeared ghost-like. Her eyes wavered from the glass briefly, glancing through Poppy. She appeared washed out, as if she had been repeatedly soaped and scrubbed and wringed to the point where all her colours had faded.

"Hi," Poppy smiled, hoping her uneasiness was not obvious.

"This is Arabella," Edith introduced. Arabella's pale eyes had already drifted back to the glass case and the object within it, but she lifted a small, white hand in a wave. She must be a porcelain doll, Poppy thought, that's why she can't move too much or too quickly.

Glancing at Edith, she waited for her to guide the conversation or at least lead her into another room. But Edith only stood with her hands folded, her face patiently expectant.

Poppy took a step forward, simultaneously apprehensive and curious of the strange girl, "I'm Poppy. I'm a friend of your – oh," she caught a glance of the object that Arabella was looking at. It was a mask, but a startingly realistic imitation of Arabella's face, down to the exact location of the freckles across the nose. Poppy felt a dense ball of dread form in the pit of her stomach. There was something terribly wrong with this mask.

"That's you," she said dumbly.

Arabella shook her head sadly. She pressed her fingertips against the glass, as if she could simply push her hand through.

"Did you make it?"

"You could say that," Edith's voice startled Poppy, "Come along now Arabella, leave it alone. Come have tea with us,"

Arabella dutifully pulled herself away from the mask, treading softly through a door. Edith waved at Poppy to follow before closing the door behind them.

"Please take a seat, make yourself comfortable,"

Poppy perched on the edge of an armchair, uncomfortably aware of the grandeur that surrounded her. The material of the seat was like silk, bordered by a rich, mahogany wood. She felt severely out of place in her cotton skirt and blouse. The room itself was frozen in time, filled with dark furniture and littered with antiques.

She nervously eyed the petite tea set on the low coffee table. Fragile bone china was delicately painted with flourishing flowers. Poppy was convinced they would smash if she dared touch one. She watched fascinated as Edith picked up the tea pot with elongated, bony fingers and poured two cups of tea through dainty strainers. She deftly poured a drop of milk in each cup and placed one before Poppy and the second before herself.

Poppy just assumed Arabella did not like tea.

Edith abruptly launched into conversation, completely

ignoring any niceties such as small talk. Poppy stiffened at the sudden onslaught of questions, "Can you tell me exactly what the man you saw looked like please? Such as his clothes, his face, roughly what his age could be? I want to be completely sure that it is Joseph,"

Poppy guardedly answered Edith's questions. She was conscious that this woman may already know certain things and she did not want to present herself as a key source of information. She planned to keep this as her only visit to the Morris household. She was, however, slightly infuriated by the fact that her previous description had seemingly been disregarded.

"You said he created flames?"

"Yes," Poppy glanced at Arabella, attempting to gauge the family dynamics. Was Arabella aware of her family's history? Or had she been kept in the dark like Travis? She needn't have worried, Arabella had the vague look of someone completely lost in their own mind.

"That sounds awfully like him, using his powers to scare off a child,"

A child? Poppy felt her cheeks flush with indignation. She was not a child.

"I think you need to talk to Travis about this," Poppy suggested, "He's seen him way more often than me and I really feel like this isn't my business,"

Several emotions flitted across Edith's features: surprise, anger, despondency, "I miss my grandson, I haven't seen him in so many years," Edith lamented, "I don't even know what kind of ability he has developed," Edith stared hard at Poppy, once again an expectant look on her face.

Poppy shifted awkwardly, "That's sad,"

"Yes. Quite,"

There was a pause.

"I often wonder," Edith tried again, "What he is like as a young man?"

"Uh," Poppy floundered, "He's very nice,"

"You said you were friends?"

"Only recently," Poppy lied.

"Please tell me more about him," Edith began to beg to Poppy's horror, "Is he tall? Short? Thin? Fat? What is his ability? What is he like?"

He's beautiful Poppy almost blurted. A blush furiously burned her cheeks and she picked up her tea, staring steadfastly into it, "He's quite tall and he has dark hair, and he thinks he wants to work with animals,"

"Animals?"

"Yes," Poppy managed an awkward laughed, "Like elephants. He turned one orange once…"

Edith's brows knitted together in confusion, "I don't understand," she said quietly. Poppy internally admonished herself, sensing a sudden menace in Edith's voice. Why was that elephant always on her mind?

"Travis is a Chromatophoric Kinaesthetic," she clarified, acting as if it was a perfectly reasonable explanation.

"Oh," a brief look of what she could have sworn was disappointment crossed Edith's face.

"What about you?"

Poppy ducked her head, building her courage to respond with a clear 'I'm powerless', when the uncomfortable quietness was shattered by an unearthly wail. The sound reverberated around the room, rattling paintings on the walls. It crawled into Poppy's ears, viciously digging into her ear drums. She clutched her hands to her head, the noise so loud if was painful. It seemed to suck the air from her lungs and simultaneously crush her with its sorrow.

Bean sídhe.

Banshee.

The phrase rose unbidden in Poppy's mind. As a child, her Grandmother has regaled her with terrifying tales of banshees. Their howls were feared; they were said to warn of upcoming disaster and death. But they were just folklore from her Grandmother's homeland, they weren't real. Were they?

Edith leapt clumsily to her feet, struggling to physically push against the sound. She shouted something that may have been "I'll be right back," but Poppy could not be sure. Arabella looked at the ceiling dauntingly, her fingertips pressed firmly into her ears.

After what felt like an eternity, the wail ceased, and silence chased the beating force of the noise out of the room. Poppy gasped for breath, once again picking up the dainty teacup with trembling hands. The cup conspicuously rattled against the saucer, so she returned it to the table.

"Who is your friend?"

"Sorry?" Poppy coughed. She jumped in surprise at Arabella's voice. It was soft and fleeting, as if the words wanted to spend as little time in the air as possible.

"You said 'I'm a friend of your'. What did you mean?"

Poppy frantically searched her memory for what she might have said to Arabella. It arrived quickly, having said so little to Arabella in the hallway before she had been distracted by the mask, "Oh, I was saying that I was a friend of your cousin's,"

"Travis? How is he?"

Arabella obviously had not been listening to her and Edith's conversation. But she felt more confident, preparing herself to regurgitate exactly what she had said to Edith.

Instead, different words fell out, "I feel quite bad that he can't be here, actually. I'm in a bit of a weird position to be honest," she admitted, "Being able to visit and talk to you guys when he's not allowed. It's strange. But Travis is really good. He mentioned that you visited him?"

Arabella nodded, the ghost of a smile tugging at her lips. Poppy took this as encouragement and continued, "Yeah, he said that he remembers playing with you when he was little, and that he had fun," She was lying, but only a little bit.

Arabella had perked up, "Does he remember-"

She was suddenly interrupted by another deafening wail.

Poppy clutched the arms of the chair, her nails digging into the soft fabric, "What is that?" she shouted.

Arabella clambered heavily to her feet and laboriously reached over to Poppy, grabbing her by the wrist, "I'll show you," she mouthed.

Poppy reluctantly allowed herself to be dragged up the stairs by Arabella. Unbidden images conjured by her Grandmother's stories assaulted her mind. Pale, gaunt faces enclosed in swathes of black shadows, pulled and tugged into expressions of horror.

The closer they got to the source of the noise, the harder it was to move against the force of the sound. Tendrils of sorrow and despair were entangled within a sheer wall of anger. It roiled around their heads and bodies, trying to push them back down the stairs.

"I'm not allowed to see her when she's like this," Arabella anxiously shouted over her shoulder, "I make her worse. But you need to see, you need to help,"

"How?" Poppy cried back. She was struggling to breathe and catch the wild tangle of her thoughts. They kept slipping from her. Why was she here? How was she supposed to help? What was making that noise?

When they reached the top of the staircase, a door hung open, disrupting the soundproofing of the room. The noise was emanating from inside, erupting from the doorway in waves. Poppy pushed alongside Arabella, holding a hand before her face in an attempt to batter away the noise. She felt she was forcing herself against the gale of a hurricane, pushing towards the centre of the storm.

Inside, a woman lay twisting and writhing in her bed sheets. Edith clung to her, shouting words, but her voice was lost in the tumult of emotions. The woman's hair was plastered to her forehead, but she shared the same features as Arabella. Arabella hid behind the wall, leaning heavily against it, leaving Poppy alone in the doorway.

"It's my mother," she shouted, "Her name is Margaret. Help her!"

Poppy began to discern words amongst the screams and shrieks.

"Where is my daughter? Where is my Bella?" Margaret screamed.

"She's calling for you!" Poppy realised. She grabbed Arabella's elbow, pulling her into the room. Edith yelled something at them from Margaret's bedside, her face contorted in a mask of anger. Poppy ignored her and continued dragging the ghostly girl, pushing breathlessly against the oncoming tide.

They stopped, falling to their knees in an attempt to stay still. They crawled to the bedside. Margaret caught sight of Arabella and began pulling away from Edith towards her, "Bee! My sweetheart, come here my Bumble Bee!"

The strength of the noise ebbed, and Poppy felt she was finally able to think. As Margaret gripped Arabella's hands, Edith grabbed Poppy's, firmly placing them onto the cool flannel on Margaret's forehead.

Please be calm, Poppy thought desperately, please stop screaming.

"Bee, where's Bella?" Margaret suddenly looked desperate. Her eyes rolled around the room and settled sightlessly again on Arabella, "Where is she Bee?" She reached out, almost clawing at Arabella's face, "She's not here, where is she?"

"She's here!" Poppy blurted, struggling to keep her voice soft and soothing in the sudden onslaught of sound. Arabella's eyes watered, and she could only shake her head noiselessly.

"She's holding your hands right now," Poppy continued, turning to Edith in panic. Edith was fiddling with a pill bottle, fumbling against the child-safety lid. She nodded encouragingly at Poppy, waving her hand in the universal symbol of keep going!

"She's going to help you get to sleep," Poppy scrabbled for something to say, "Because you're tired and we're all tired and Arabella's here, she's here, you're fine, she's here, we're all here for some reason,"

The words tumbled out in a repetitive stream, but they seemed to be working. The pressure of the sound on them began to recede, the blood was no longer thundering in their temples. Margaret slowly stopped her writhing, and Edith wrapped her firmly in her sheets, feeding her tablets with shaking hands.

Poppy continued murmuring in a soft voice, attempting a soothing and peaceful tone. Despite the tumult of anxious emotions in her mind, her own words seemed to be working on her. She felt something changing inside, as if something was finally clicking into place. She sensed a new sensation in her own body. She drew on it, and Margaret grew calmer and calmer. Eventually Poppy could do no more and her head flopped onto the edge bed in exhaustion.

Arabella refused to let go of her mother's hands until she was fast asleep.

CHAPTER 11
27th October 2019

A week later, Poppy found herself ensconced within the expensive armchair in the Morris' front room. She sat facing Edith, leaning forward in disbelief at the words emanating from her in those soft but authoritative tones.

"Some abilities are so natural, so engrained within our systems that they aren't always perceptible. In your case, you rarely had occasion to employ your ability and therefore you did not even know you had it," Edith laughed, as if it was a witty joke.

To Poppy it was not a joke. It was an epiphany. A horror. A complete world-altering discovery.

She had powers.

It pushed so many aspects of her life into redundancy. The doctor's appointments, the therapy sessions, her self-image. How had Dr Thackery, a literal trained professional, got it wrong? She hated herself for the relief she felt; she wasn't so different after all.

"So Organic Kinaesthesis?" was all she could muster.

"The ability to manipulate organic matter and cells," Edith confirmed, dropping a sugar cube into her black tea, and stirring it with a miniscule teaspoon, "That includes the standard animal and plant cells, but also organic compounds such as hormones. Hence your ability to calm my daughter down last week and your ability to grow exceptional plants,"

Poppy nodded, dumbfounded. She was still struggling to come to terms with the idea. But there was a small bud in her brain, a flourish of excitement that was itching to experiment.

"I can see you're eager to try it out," Edith said warmly.

Poppy nodded vigorously.

Edith retrieved a small succulent plant from the ornate mantel piece and placed it carefully in the centre of the coffee table. She precisely measured it with a ruler, announcing it was three and a half centimetres.

"Let's see if you can get it a bit taller," she suggested.

Poppy gently placed her fingertips on the thick, fleshy leaves. Unsure what to expect, she found herself disappointed by the fact that she could not sense anything at all. A panicky feeling quickly rolled into her mind uninvited, like a bank of thunderous clouds on a summer afternoon. What if Edith was playing a particularly cruel joke? What if she didn't have powers after all?

Memories of her early visits to Dr Thackery, and the feelings of bewilderment they often still evoked, assaulted her. She glanced at Edith helplessly, frightened that she was making a fool of herself in front of such a formidable woman.

But suddenly! There! She could sense a small movement beneath the surface of the leaves, like water pumping through a pipe. Except it was not water. It was an energy. An energy she could move around at will.

A soft breath escaped her as she pushed and tugged gently at the energy, reminded of her plants at home. Is this what she had been doing the entire time? Had her 'gardening thoughts' actually had power behind them? So entranced by this new feeling, she failed to notice Edith's expression transform into pure glee.

Poppy continued to manipulate the flow, suggesting that it drift upwards and outwards. She heard a whistle of air through teeth, and a felt a quivering beneath her fingers. But it was tiring. To push the flow, she had to draw from her own strength reserves. Her strength drained unexpectedly quickly. With so little practice, she had little idea of how to pace herself.

So, with a gasp, she stopped. Sweat beaded on her brow. The succulent plant had grown outwards as well as up, causing a fracture to form in the pot as the plant strained against its confines.

Edith's hands fluttered to her neck in delight, "That was extraordinary," she gushed, "It's rare you see this much potential,"

"Do you know many Organic Kinaesthetics?" Poppy asked, wiping the sweat away with her sleeve. She gulped water from the crystal glass Edith had given her on her arrival. It flowed coolly down her throat, relieving the sudden dehydration.

"Oh, uh, some," Edith nodded. She expected her to continue, but Edith avoided eye contact as she refilled Poppy's empty glass from a water jug.

"What are they like?" she pushed, "Did they find out late like me?"

"I really wouldn't know," Edith responded sharply, "Now, try it without touching it,"

"Oh, I'm not sure I can-"

She was interrupted by the harsh thump of glass against wood as Edith forcefully replaced the water jug on the table, "Really Poppy!" she snapped, "You cannot give up so easily!"

Poppy abruptly pulled her hands away from the succulent, unnerved by Edith's outburst. She sat on her hands so there was no chance of her touching the plant again. When she concentrated, she could still sense the plant, albeit a far weaker signal. She half-heartedly tried, but knew she was getting nowhere. She was distracted, half-concerned by the fact Edith had refused to answer her questions. She would have to undertake her own research. The plant drooped sadly, feeling her exhaustion as it seeped deeply into her bones.

Edith tutted disappointedly when the succulent failed to grow again, "I am going to have to get a fresh pot," she muttered sorrowfully.

"I'm sorry," Poppy apologised, "But I should probably get going,"

Quickly gathering her coat and scarf, she loudly glugged some more water from her glass. Edith's watch of the succulent did not faulter as Poppy pulled her coat on. It was as she was leaving that she felt a sudden weight on her shoulders and chest. A weight so great it seemed to push her into the ground so that she could no longer move. She strained against it and a feeling of panic bloomed in her chest when she found she couldn't take another step.

"You will come back, won't you Poppy?" Edith's voice was cold. Poppy managed to turn her head just enough to see Edith's eyes boring into her.

"Of course," Poppy stuttered, straining against the crushing force.

"Do you have something to say?"

"Thank you, Miss Morris," Poppy's voice emerged strangled. The weight had grown unbearable. She realised it was Edith. She was crushing her. Killing her.

"You're welcome, Poppy," the hand that rested on the small of her back withdrew the excruciating crushing sensation. She was finally able to move again, able to breathe.

"And please," Edith said as she showed Poppy out, "Call me Edith,"

...

"She did what?" Travis exclaimed.
"Oh Travis, it was awful!" Poppy rubbed at her eyes.

They ached, uncomfortably tight now that the tears had dried, "I am so grateful to her, honestly. Of course, I am! For revealing this about me, but I can't bear go back there!"

Travis swiftly embraced Poppy, pulling her into a tight hug right there on his doorstep. She had come to him straight away, a nervous ball of fear, anger, and excitement. He was stunned at her revelation, had never heard of an Organic Kinaesthetic. He had repeated the phrase several times, testing the new name in his mouth. But when Poppy had finally finished, he suddenly had an understanding as to why his mother had turned her back on Edith.

Poppy's head rested on his chest, and Travis found himself frozen to the doorstep. He wanted to remain in this moment, with her hair tickling his cheek and her smell sticking to his clothes. He wanted to draw her inside, hide her and hold her and keep her safe.

But Joseph was lurking in the living room doorway and Travis was forced to remember his promise.

Poppy allowed herself to be drawn in Travis' arms. She could feel his warmth on her cheek, sense his flow of energy through his body. She felt safe, for the first time since she had arrived at Edith's house. She hoped he would invite her in, away from the cold of his doorstep.

She pulled away from him, suddenly awkward but hopeful.

"I can't invite you in," he said abruptly, as if he knew what she was thinking. He took a step back, across the threshold of the door, "I'm sorry. If you let me grab a coat, we can go somewhere?"

"Yeah, okay," Poppy agreed, but as he turned away, she blurted out, "If she wants me to go back, will you come?"

He stepped back towards her, "Poppy, you know I can't–"

But suddenly she couldn't hear him anymore.

"Travis?" she said loudly, "Travis, I can't hear you?" She reached out, confused that she could still hear traffic on the road and birds in the trees, but Travis' mouth was moving without making a sound. Her hand hit something, an invisible wall, and she realised there was something separating them.

Travis was shouting silently, as if trapped in a soundproof box. He was smacking the invisible wall with his palms as Poppy, desperate and bewildered, ran her hands over the invisible force. She noticed that Travis was no longer shouting at her, but at something over her shoulder.

She whirled around to find his mother there, her hands clenched into fists above dropped shopping bags, her face twisted into a furious snarl.

Travis relentlessly hit the wall his mother had summoned, throwing his shoulder against it, continuing to shout despite his voice becoming hoarse, "You can't do this! Drop the wall Mum! Drop it! Don't listen to her Poppy!" He knew it was of no use, neither of them could hear him, but his desperation prevented him from stopping.

His commotion attracted Joseph from the gloominess of the living room. He insisted on keeping the curtains closed to the front garden now, his paranoia of an invisible enemy getting the best of him. Despite shaving, his stubble was already beginning to grow back. He stood cautiously in the shadows, unwilling to enter full view of the doorway.

"What the hell is going on?" he hissed.

"She's blocked me out!" Travis yelled, "She's built this wall so I can't talk to Poppy!" He gave the wall one more furious punch with his fist, but it had no effect. He rested his forehead against the invisible force field. It buzzed softly, like the window of a bus when it was idling at a traffic light. He watched hopelessly as Anna berated Poppy to the soundtrack of his own heavy breathing.

"She has no right," he mumbled as he watched Poppy tearfully shake her head, then turn and run. His chest bloomed with anger as Joseph rested a hand on his shoulder, "She's just being protective,"

"Protective?" Travis shrugged off his hand, "Why do I need protecting from her?" He watched hopelessly as Poppy ran from his mother, furious that this decision was being made for him.

Anna dropped her wall just in time to hear the door to her son's bedroom slam.

CHAPTER 12
28th October 2019

The evening had rolled in unexpectedly quickly, catching trailing school children off guard as they dawdled home from school, making them hurry back to their bright houses, warm beacons in the dark. By seven, the streets were almost deserted, except for the occasional lone dog walker.

The night was unusually mild, so that Poppy and Aaron only wore jumpers as they hurried along the pavement. The sky was littered with stars. It seemed to Poppy as if it were a thick, velvet blanket that someone had poked countless holes in to reveal a bright, shining, inaccessible world beyond.

"How far is it?" she asked worriedly as they traversed across town. She was uncomfortably aware that this was the path she usually took to the Morris home.

"Quite far, beyond the Morris' though, if that's what you're worried about," Aaron responded, digging his hands into his pockets.

Poppy had related to him what had happened. He had remained suspiciously quiet, had not even asked her to demonstrate her ability, and only reluctantly agreed to letting her tag along to one of his mysterious meetings in the hope she could see Travis. But there was no guarantee he would be there this time.

He hadn't attended the past two meetings.

She was struggling to comprehend all these new feelings, a tumultuous ball of raw emotion in her chest. She found herself furious with her old counsellor, her early teachers, even her parents. Possibly mostly at herself. How had she gotten through so many years without knowing?

At the moment however, she was hurt by the fact that Aaron seemed unbothered by her capability. She decided to show him, perhaps that would inject some enthusiasm into him.

"Hey Aaron, I haven't shown you my power yet," she announced.

"No, I guess not," he attempted a look of excitement, but his face only looked strained.

"Well, I'll show you right now!" What was he so worried about? Did he think she would show him up? The thought niggled uncomfortably at her, surely he wasn't that selfish?

She looked around for something suitably impressive. She had been practicing all week, as if building up to the big performance for her brother. Settling on a relatively young pine sapling, barely taller than herself, she stalked over to it determinedly.

"Ready?" she called. She did not wait for his response.

Placing her palms on the rough bark, she felt the surficial grooves and knots of the tree trunk. Beneath that, she could sense a current, like what she thought Mallory could feel with electricity. It darted up and down the length of the tree, deep within the confines of its cells. She followed the current, letting her mind connect in serpent-like tendrils, and began to guide them to her will.

The tree began to tilt, reluctantly at first but more fluidly the further it bent. The current sparked, objecting to being disrupted in such a stark manner, but she was able to continue pushing until the tree was bent at a perfect right angle. Growth of bark accommodated the outer side of the curve and the tree looked like it had voluntarily grown in that exact position.

Aaron gaped in astonishment as Poppy allowed the tree to return to its natural position.

"Isn't that cool?" she grinned, panting with excitement and exhaustion, "I can manipulate the... the," her fingers clutched at the air as she grasped for the right word, "life force of living things and guide them to do what I want!"

She stopped suddenly, stunned by the horror in her brother's eyes.

"What is it?" she asked, the hurt obvious in her voice. Why wasn't he impressed? Although she would be loathed to admit it, finally having a power was the most liberating thing that had ever happened to her. No longer was she an outcast, an inscrutable person. Yet ever since she had told him, Aaron seemed guarded, scared even.

"Living things," his voice cracked, "Does that include people?"

"Of course not!" she retorted defensively, but she felt a sudden blooming fear in her chest. Uninvited thoughts of Travis' mother bombarded her vision. Anna had told her she was no longer welcome, no longer allowed near her son if she was associating with Edith. She had called her dangerous. She had insinuated that Poppy wanted to hurt Travis.

She had chosen to ignore her, so certain that this wasn't true. But what if Anna was right? What if she hurt him even by accident?

"But it does! You have the ability to manipulate people!"

"I wouldn't do that!" She took a pleading step towards him, but he backed away from her into the road. Was this it? Was she to be outcast in a completely different sense? She had failed to research her own power like she had promised herself, too wrapped up in physically experimenting. She felt she was missing something, a vital piece of a pictureless puzzle.

She heard the engine of a car, and a new fear gripped her.

"Aaron get out of the road!" she shouted. However, he didn't listen, too distracted by what he had just witnessed. The car's engine grew louder, and Poppy rushed forward to pull him out of the road.

"Don't come near me!" In a panic, Aaron fired a wall of vibrating sound particles into her. She flew backwards, tripping on the curb and landing on her back. She was too slow to clamber back to her feet as the car hurtled around the corner and-

Screeched to a vicious halt.

The headlights caught them like prey, and furiously brightened.

In the centre of the road, Aaron swore under his breath, "It's Mallory,"

Mallory clambered out from the driver's seat, buzzing with anger. The headlights, fuelled by her fury, illuminating the entire road.

The elongated, skeletal shadows of the trees shivered as Mallory yelled, "Get in the car!"

Aaron sulkily did as he was told, collapsing in the back seat, eager to get away from the twin who was suddenly so alien to him.

Poppy did not move. She couldn't move. She was stuck to the curb, her body shaking, confused by the countless emotions currently running amok in her mind.

Mallory marched over, "Do you know how worried Mum and Dad are right now? They're also driving around town looking for you both,"

She looked up at her sister tearfully, "Sorry, I was trying to see Travis but…" she trailed off, her bottom lip trembling as she tried to control herself.

Mallory paused, surprised by her apparent remorse. She crouched down beside her, "Pop, it's okay now we've found you,"

"Aaron hates me," she blurted, pressing the heels of her hands into her eyes.

"What? Why?"

Poppy unhappily explained what had just happened. Mallory, astounded that her sister had manifested an ability, managed to bite her togue and not interrupt. She instantly understood the implications, her face becoming grim.

"Let's get you into the car and home," she said gently, "We'll sort this,"

"Please don't tell Mum and Dad," Poppy begged, "I couldn't stand it if they hated me too,"

"That's a problem for tomorrow,"

She slid into the back seat of the car beside her brother. Aaron stubbornly stared out of the window, refusing to acknowledge her presence. Mallory turned the ignition key and the car rumbled to life. As she pulled away from the curb and turned around, she had mixed feelings. She had indirectly helped her sister discover her ability, by revealing Poppy's story at school. She really hadn't had much choice in that. She had learned of the stigma attached to such a power years ago. Would it have been better if she had never learned about it at all?

She regularly glanced in the rear-view mirror, watching her siblings obstinately ignore one another. Eventually, the silence got to her.

"Poppy's power is an amazing thing," she announced icily, "It may not have been the one we wanted her to have, but the fact she has one after all these years is incredible,"

Poppy stared ashamedly into her lap. She had been so happy to have finally been blessed, but from the way everyone was talking, it was obviously more of a curse.

"Poppy is still learning about everything that's associated with her ability," Mallory continued, "Aaron, you gotta have some sympathy here, we went through this when were, like, seven,"

"Yeah, and we were properly told how to not hurt anyone," Aaron responded.

"I know how to not hurt anyone!" Poppy interjected.

"Do you know how not to control someone?" he demanded.

"I am not going to control you stupid!"

"How do I know you're not doing it right now?"

"Because I'm your sister!" her voice wavered with anguish at the fact her brother thought she would even think she would take advantage of him like that.

"I don't think it's possible to fake your kind of stupid Aaron," Mallory added from the driver's seat. She swerved the car into their drive, jolting them to a halt. She released her seatbelt and whirled around to face Aaron.

"Seriously, you're acting like a dick," she hissed, jabbing him in the shoulder with an electrified finger, "Stop it,"

He flinched away, before throwing the car door open and storming into the house. Mallory and Poppy watched in silence as, lit up by the car headlights, he threw them the finger. Poppy felt deflated.

"Will everyone respond like this Mal?" she asked sadly. She realised how much she still had to learn. All the lessons she had missed out on as a child.

Mallory sighed, rubbing her eyes, "Maybe,"

CHAPTER 13
6th November 2019

On her return from school, Poppy rushed out into the garden. Being trapped in her lessons had made her itchy, and it was difficult to restrain herself from using her abilities on anything at school. She did not want anyone else to find out just yet, especially her schoolmates. They all knew about her powerlessness. It would be twisted into something ugly if they found out, especially since there was such a stigma attached. She was convinced rumours would spread: rumours saying she deliberately hid her ability so she could be special or rumours saying she had manipulated her way through school.

She stood in the centre of the garden, wondering which plant to practice on first. Being in the school corridors made her dizzy now that she could tune into everyone's energy. They were difficult to grasp for her untrained ability however, even if she had wanted to. Plants were easier. Plants were safe. Plants weren't people.

She found herself in the greenhouse, a long trough of

bell pepper plants displaying late produce. She held a pepper in her hands, pushing and pushing with her mind, delighted at the swelling of the vegetable. She grinned impishly, letting it go.

It swung briefly, but was too heavy and bloated. The momentum of the swollen pepper pulled the entire plant forwards and off the shelf. It crashed to the floor, the pot shattering and soil spraying across the floor. The pepper had splattered, destroyed by its own weight. Its internal juices mixed in ugly swirls with the scattered soil.

Poppy felt her stomach roll over sickeningly. Aaron's fear returned to her. If she was this careless with plants, what other damage could she cause?

"Poppy?"

She jumped at the sound of her mother's voice. Claire frowned at the mess, "What have you done here?"

"Sorry, just being clumsy," she lied. She had still yet to tell her parents of her newly discovered ability. This thing inside her was unready, premature. Each time she shared it there had been poor consequences. But it was also gnawing at her insides, filling her limbs with a trembling excitement and disbelief with its mere existence.

But she had not realised the distance her power had travelled through the trough.

"These weren't this big yesterday," Claire muttered, gently plucking another pepper from a plant further down. Poppy turned, to her horror she saw the entire row of plants were displaying bulging produce. Her stomach fluttered, had she done that?

Claire turned to her daughter, disbelief written into the crevices on her face, "How did this happen?" She immediately caught the sheepish glint in her eye. Her mouth gaped open, "Did you do this?"

"I er…"

Claire gripped her by the shoulders, her nails digging into Poppy's school shirt, "Poppy, do you have powers?"

Poppy nodded. She tensed, uncertain of how her

ESSENCE

mother would react. Would she be like Aaron? Disgusted by the implications of these abilities? Claire cradled the pepper in her palm, then she suddenly hurtled out of the greenhouse and across the garden, hollering for her husband.

Patrick appeared blurry eyed, "What's going on?"

"She's got powers Pat," Claire's words came out in a rush as she waved the bell pepper in his face, "Poppy's got powers,"

...

On his return from school, Travis retreated to his bedroom like he had done every day that week. He tried projecting some cool, calming patterns on his bedroom wall but his frustration repeatedly overwhelmed it, changing the patterns into something confusing and turning the colours murky. He settled on listening to music whilst trying to focus on his homework.

He heard the tentative knock on his door. In response he pulled his headphones more firmly over his ears, maxing out the volume. His head dipped to the beat as he scrawled algebra across the page. His thoughts were drifting, however, to schemes that would allow him to see Poppy. Mikey and Benji had given him some good ideas, and they were willing to help buy him some time so he could at least talk to her.

A sudden, unexpected hand was on his shoulder. Travis flinched, elbowing a glass of water across his homework. He leapt to his feet as water dribbled onto his trousers, dashing to grab tissues in an attempt to save his work.

Joseph stood awkwardly, the bedroom door swinging open behind him, "I'm sorry, I didn't mean to make you jump,"

Travis silently wiped up the mess, music blasting tinnily from the headphones around his neck.

"Look, I've come to speak about something important,"

Joseph pushed, "I need you to stop wiping that and sit down and listen!" Joseph grabbed the damp tissues from Travis, throwing them aside.

Travis squeezed the bridge of his nose in exasperation, still not used to the fact that this stranger had made himself so comfortable in his house.

"Fine," he mumbled reluctantly, turning the music off and slumping onto his bed. He hoped Joseph would leave soon, he felt uncomfortable in his presence.

Joseph did not sit. Instead, he stood erect, as if standing to attention.

"I heard you talkin' to that lass the other day," he began, "And there is something not right about her,"

Travis remained stony faced, restraining himself from responding with 'Oh brilliant, you too,'. It seemed like his family were determined to drive a wedge between him and Poppy.

"The whole situation is fishy to me," he claimed, "There's nothing natural about a girl who claims to grow up powerless only to discover an extraordinary ability by any standard with the help of a woman like Edith Morris,"

"What are you trying to say?" Travis felt a hot, burning lump of anger in his chest. At Joseph's words it flared and tightened around his lungs. There was shame there too, shame that these thoughts had already occurred to him. There was certainly something strange about this whole situation.

Joseph began pacing, anxiously running a hand through his grey hair, "What do you know about Organic Kinaesthetics?"

Travis shrugged, "They have the ability to manipulate organic matter?" he offered. He knew precious little else, what with his internet privileges being severely limited.

Joseph shuddered to a stop and stared at him, "You understand what that entails right?"

Without breaking eye contact, Travis shrugged again.

"Right, consider this. A man is born with the ability to

control anything organic. Muscles, cells, hormones, feelings. Now that man is talented at growing plants. He can manipulate the cells of the plants so that they grow bigger and better. He wonders if he can do the same for his dogs. He quickly discovers that he can stop his dogs from doing anything he doesn't want them to. He can stop them from chewing the furniture or running off. That's not too bad, is it? But then he starts doing the same to his children,"

Beads of sweat began to form on Travis' forehead. It seemed like quite the jump from plants to dogs to children, but he understood the point Joseph was trying to make. He felt pinned beneath his great uncle's intense gaze, and was unnerved by the story, "You knew someone like that, didn't you?"

"These abilities are rare for a reason," was all Joseph said.

"But Poppy isn't like that!" he argued, "I've known her for years, she's never been controlling,"

"People change. I've seen enough of it. Under pressure and stress, people will do terrible things. It all ends the same…" Joseph's eyes glazed over, and his hands were shaking. A heat began emanating from him. His voice grew quiet, and the words slipped out in a rush, "So many people. So many hurt and injured by an Organic's control,"

He fell to his knees and gripped Travis' hands, "You need to stay away from her. You can never know if she's controlling you or not,"

Joseph's palms were burning his hands, causing Travis to hiss through his teeth in pain.

"Stay away. They've got her now, you can't help her,"

"But what if I can?" he argued, trying to pull his hands away. His wrists and palms were burning, he could smell the flesh. In desperation, he shouted "Let go!"

Joseph did, muttering to himself. He stumbled about the room, rubbing his scalp again with burning hands. Travis hurtled to the door, screaming for his mother. By the time Anna reached his room, Joseph had already collapsed.

Part 2
Joseph

ESSENCE

CHAPTER 1
26/11/2019

Police Transcripts:
The following transcript was recorded on Saturday 25th November 2019. It is evidence that will have significant impact on the Morris case, dated August 1979. This interview was led by Detective Inspector Anthony Morales and Sergeant Tim Jones. The interviewee is Dr Joseph Morris, supported by his niece Anna Lee.

...

DI: The time of commencement is 18:01. Mr Morris, you are here under the suspicion of causing destruction to the Morris Estate property following the events of today, and also under the suspicion of murder in relation to your brother Nathaniel Morris. We're going to begin with Nathaniel's death. It is our understanding that, after he died, you effectively disappeared for 40 years. Can you explain the events that occurred during this time?

Morris: That's a loaded question, a lot happened during

that time.

DI: Okay, let's start at the beginning then. Your brother was just murdered, you were accused of the crime. You ran. Why? Why didn't you come to the police?

Morris: Having abandoned the scene, it looked suspicious, and I felt I couldn't go back without being falsely accused and sentenced. At the time, I valued my sister-in-law's opinion. She told me how bad it looked, and I believed her.

DI: Can you explain what happened after you left the estate?

...

17th August 1979

Joseph's memory is limited. He barely remembers that night anymore. He glimpses only flashes. Edith's face. The towering trees black against the navy sky. The conviction that his skin was melting as he was trapped amongst the flames. The little he can recall is billowing smoke between skeletal branches, the suffocating silence of the forest that eventually morphed into the roaring of the River Magnus.

His skin is burning, he can feel it peeling away, layer by crisp layer. There is a moaning, a low animalistic sound. Where is it coming from? Are there creatures in this forest? Is somebody hurt? There is noise all around him, the crackling of flames punctuated with the sound of rending metal. But all through that is the consistent sound of desolate moaning.

There are wispy shapes of soldiers amongst the trees. Shadow figures that vanish into tendrils of smoke. Are these his comrades? All the soldiers he had tried to help but failed? Have they come back for him?

With the orange glow of the flames behind him, like a

blazing setting sun, he walks forwards into the darkness. The noise of the burning becomes muted, absorbed by the wood and leaves. Deeper into its depths, the forest is damper. There hasn't been rain for days, but here deep in the woods it is still damp. The leaves are too full of moisture to curl in the heat radiating from him.

There is that moaning. The sound clearer now.

The soldiers are calling. Calling him forwards. Perhaps guiding him to the source of the moaning, the creature that is in desperate need of his help. He runs and they are running beside him, whispering shadows that slide through the trees. Boots thump against the forest floor, a hypnotic, steady rhythm. They are shouting at him, but he can't tell if they are angry or despairing.

He runs further into the night. The moaning is drumming against his ears. It reminds him of all those soldiers, lying and awaiting their ends in orderly rows. Even until the end, they were orderly. He pulls the rough fabric of the blanket back, the material scrapes between his fingertips. It reveals a young boy, barely old enough to be here at all. He is a sufferer of the Morris Mios, he can see it in the dilation of his eyes, the ragged gasps of his breathing, the burns on his skin. He can't do anything for the poor soul. There is nothing that can stop this atrocity.

Unless...

If he could stop his brother...

The soldier is ahead of him now, that young boy that was still pockmarked with acne when he died. He is leading him between the trees, running and shouting and desperate. The moaning is so clear now, they must be upon the poor creature, surely?

Yet the soldiers beside him, that had been running in time with him, they were no longer there. Now he was running with wolves, alongside big black dogs with burning scarlet eyes, pools of blood like those that so often puddled the floor in the infirmary. They overwhelm his vision, and he feels himself drowning, lost to the bottomless pools of blood.

They are roaring. These cruel creatures that remind him of his failures, of all the boys he had failed to save, they are howling and roaring and his skin is burning. He realises now, the moaning is emanating from his own throat. He is the one in need of saving, from his monsters surrounding him, from the flames that are burning beneath his skin.

The roaring. It is actually the roaring of flowing water. He is standing on an outcrop. Dried loose soil crunches beneath his boots, desiccated from the long, rainless summer. The black wolves are behind him, their eyes alight with the fire he has caused. They growl and morph into lost soldiers and they crowd forward, each desperate to touch him, to feel him, to take his soul as penance.

Joseph stumbles back, a step too far. The outcrop collapses, spilling him and his burning body into the cool, encompassing waters of the Magnus.

CHAPTER 2
26/11/2019

DI: Upon Nathaniel's death, it was his will and testament that his company should go to you. Is this correct?

Morris: Yes. But obviously that didn't happen because he signed the company over to Io Technologies literal seconds before his death.

DI: Did you murder your brother to gain control of the company?

Morris: No! Of course not! Why would I kill him after he signed the company over to someone else?

DI: We have evidence that you gained a role within the acquired Morris company in March 1983 under the fake name Malcolm Brendanowicz. Is this true?

Morris: Yes.

DI: So, if not due to obsession of owning your brother's

legacy, why did you join the company?

...

March 1983

A newspaper flutters in the sheltered doorway of an Irish Bar. It is dated March 1982, the headline announces that E.T. the Extra Terrestrial has been granted the People's Choice Award for Favourite Motion Picture. Another headline declares drops in stocks for Io Technologies after the production of Morris Mios was banned three months before. But someone has roughly torn this headline beneath their boots.

The tavern is dark. He basks in the gloom. The ceiling squats low over heavy, wooden furniture. Cigarette smoke curls about the dim lamps. Joseph likes this place. He enjoys the muffled silence; the jukebox had been broken for months. Tracing a finger around one of the countless rings of water stains on the bar top, he relishes the certainty of circles.

Four years. He stares dazedly into his glass, confused by its emptiness. It has been four years, give or take. He contemplates the few memories he has throughout that time. Moth-eaten couches, the cold, rough pressure of concrete against his cheek, flowing amber liquid. His mind is more often overwhelmed by images of the war. Sometimes his brother. There is little room for anything else.

He fumbles clumsily in his coat pocket for loose change. As the coins clatter onto the bar, the bell above the door tinkles. Hunched patrons barely glance up from their pints as a rowdy trio enter the tavern. They snicker at the gaudy Irish trinkets that adorn the place, smirking as they settle themselves at the bar.

The tallest of the trio orders harshly. He wears a white T-shirt beneath a black, leather jacket and is unable to prevent his hand from repeatedly running through his greased quiff. Joseph studiously ignores the Travolta wannabe, carefully counting his coins with trembling fingers.

Their voices, however, still break into his concentration, "The stocks won't stay low, my Pa says that's fact,"

"Nah, Io shouldn't have bought Morris Mios in the first place, that was the first big mistake. What use is buying a production company that can't produce what it's s'posed to?"

His ears are burning from their conversation. Joseph shifts slightly, angling himself so that he can hear them better. They are much younger than him; he realises by as much as ten years when the bartender asks for identification.

"Wrong Jimmy," Travolta jabs a weedy boy in the chest. He stumbles into Joseph, who meekly takes the hit. The information provided by this ignorant boaster could help him, and he did not want to ruin his chances by starting a fight.

"My Pa is close with the board of directors, right? He heard from this guy, Argus-"

"Argos, like the store?" the third pipes in, his voice at least an octave higher. Joseph suspects his ID is fake.

"No dummy, Ar-gus¬, he says that stocks are gonna come way back up in no time,"

"What's that Argus know about anything?" Jimmy demands.

"Well, he was the one who signed the contract with ol' Morris hisself,"

"Obviously, he's gonna say that then, isn't he?" Jimmy spits derisively.

Joseph's thoughts accelerate into overdrive. He has the vague recollection of his brother having a meeting for selling the company, he had not realised that it had taken place! How long before his death had it happened? Was it possible this Argus could know something?

He slips from the stool, abandoning his loose change

on the bar top next to his empty glass. The liquor is set into his joints, and he stumbles slightly against the doorframe. He realises, with dreaded certainty, that he will have to sober up. If he really wanted to find out what happened to his brother, he needed all the wits he could muster.

So, Joseph struggles along the cracked pavement, a plan forming in his mind. All he needed to do was find Argus.

CHAPTER 3
26/11/2019

DI: Argus is renowned on the Organic Kinaesthetic Registry as someone who repeatedly disappears off the government's radar. You are claiming that he was involved in the acquisition of the company?

Morris: Yes. I managed to meet the man fairly early on in my career there. I suspected for a long time that he was somehow involved in my brother's death. I was unable to confirm it until much later.

DI: That is quite the accusation.

Morris: My belief at the time was that Argus used his ability to force my brother to sign the contract, effectively handing over the production of the Morris Mios in their entirety, to him. We have already submitted the contract as evidence.

DI: Is that why you stayed with the company for so many years? You held quite the prominent position at one point. Did you use this position to get close to Argus?

...

September 1990

Do you remember the headlines of September 1990?
'Io Technologies illegally producing Morris Mios'
'Morris Mios Murder Continues'
'Io Technologies to be fined millions for illegal production of Morris Mios'

They are tattooed across Joseph's mind. He can easily recall the morning the first headlines were released. Restlessly straightening his tie using the reflection of the elevator doors, weary and concerned expressions mirroring his own, Styrofoam coffee cups held in trembling hands. Stepping out onto the executive floor, dodging all those panicked underwriters, stocks crashing around them. The leak to the newspaper had the potential to destroy the company unless some form of hazard mitigation was put in place. Quickly.

That was to be Joseph's role. To lead a team in building a press release. He remembers how hard it was to prevent his smile.

But he was getting ahead of himself.

His first interview with Io Technologies had taken place mere days after his overheard conversation in the Irish bar. It had failed miserably. Over a single decade fashions, technology, and interviewing styles had evolved drastically beyond his imagining. He had been underdressed compared to the other interviewees, ill-prepared for the scenario-based questions. As a result, he was not offered the role of lowly mailroom technician.

He was, however, offered the janitor role.

Setting aside pride, Joseph took it, and so began to lay the groundwork for his plan. Background checks, it seemed, were unnecessary and so Joseph was relatively safe behind his pseudonym Malcolm Brendanawicz. At work he was cheerful and friendly, known as a weak Inferno Kinaesthetic who was always willing to heat the kettle for a shared brew. A warm fellow, who everyone grew to like.

The pay was low, especially compared to the wage he was used to earning from being a military doctor. But with his first pay cheque, he was able to afford to shop in a grocery store. With his second, a deposit for a flat, albeit a grungy one. His third went towards a new suit.

Within six months of employment with Io Technologies, Joseph, or Malcolm, was working as a team leader in the mailroom. Within 12 months, he left the mailroom behind. As he rose through the ranks, his friendliness and approachability never diminished. He was popular and well thought of.

In 1989, a year of movie sequels, Joseph finally found something. He was running his own department by this point, in the marketing and media sector, a group of a dozen hardworking individuals who were loyal and dutiful.

Monday morning. He always started a Monday morning with a departmental meeting. Despite his ulterior motives, Joseph found he still had to run a department. He struggled at first with the balance, he could not let his department be so poor that he was under constant surveillance, but nor could he allow it to become so efficient that it also drew attention.

He arrives at the office early, when the sun was still struggling its way above the high-rise buildings. He feels drowsy, the dust of his sleep still crowds in the corners of his eyes. He stares at the stack of paperwork he must work through that day, the press companies he needs to contact. He worries he is losing sight of what he is here to do.

That is, until he notices the small memo tucked beneath his notepad. A request for files to be delivered at 10am on the executive floor. He rarely gets access to that infamous floor, despite his job. Being involved in the media section of the company, Joseph often gets free reign to wander into other departments in order to gain anecdotes that can be used to create good press. The executive floor, however, was always beyond his bounds.

Eventually, 9:45am rolls around. Joseph spent the entirety of his meeting with his work colleagues staring distractedly at the clock. He is finally able to excuse himself and dashes eagerly to the lift, straightening his collar and tie, and arriving on the executive floor ten minutes early.

There is a receptionist desk outside the meeting room. The young girl who usually mans it has been distracted by an executive, drawn away from her post. Joseph takes advantage, having a flick threw her notepad and also the files on the desk, but finds nothing of significance. He even checks the drawers, but finds only a magazine with the title 'How to be a successful businesswoman'.

It is as he is flicking through the magazine that he glances into the meeting room to see Argus, the secretive executive that was rarely seen, who was involved in the acquisition of his brother's company. Joseph drops the magazine back into the drawer and sidles towards the door. Through it, he is able to make out muffled voices.

"That's all for today. The next board meeting is arranged for a week tomorrow, we've got John's birthday. Oh also!" this voice is said over the scraping of chairs, "We also acknowledge that Mios will be undergoing review,"

Joseph feels his heart jolt. The mere mention of the nerve agent sends his nerves tingling, his mind tumbling into a spiral of images. The soldiers, the civilians. So many innocents suffering from that weapon.

But why were they reviewing something that had been banned so many years ago?

He is suddenly pulled from his spiral by the unexpected opening of the door. Laughs and calls tumble into the corridor and Joseph quickly allows his clenched fists to loosen and the colour gradually returns to his face. He desperately notes which directors are leaving the room: Nigel Boseman, of the accounting department; Daniel Harris of administration; Lucille Gail, a recently appointed head of human resources.

Argus is the last out of the room, and he glances distractedly at Joseph. His glasses catch the light of the florescent strip above their heads and Joseph can't quite read his expression. This is the man. The man who could hold some vital bit of information regarding his brother's death.

"Can I help you?" Argus asks.

Joseph waves the files before his face, "I have files requested from my department for a meeting here at 10am,"

Argus glances at his watch, "You're early," he comments. He looks hard at Joseph again, "Have I seen you somewhere before?

Floundering momentarily, Joseph quickly relaxes into an easy smile, "We met several years ago, when I was just in the mailroom. There are many faces down there, they don't always last long,"

"Where are you now?"

"In one of the marketing and media departments, I head the communication sector? We're the reason you've been getting such good press lately sir!"

This elicits a laugh from Argus. He slaps Joseph on the shoulder and walks away.

That was the first time Joseph heard the Io Technologies executives refer to his brother's weapon, but it certainly was not the last. He began researching, exploring the other departments led by all those directors that were crammed into the meeting that Monday morning. He investigated, subtly asking questions, teasing information out from each one. Nigel Boseman had been especially helpful after a few glasses of whisky.

Joseph finally reached a point where he was ready to act. In September 1990, he leaked documents to the press that showed, without a shadow of a doubt, that Io Technologies had continued to illegally produce Morris Mios.

Hence why, on the morning the first headlines appeared, Joseph could barely contain his glee.

CHAPTER 4
26/11/2019

DI: So you chose to take down Io Technologies from the inside?

Morris: Yes.

DI: Io Technologies almost went bankrupt several years later, most likely directly caused by your involvement. However, it did recover. Additionally, Argus was not arrested like many other directors at the company. In fact, he disappeared. I am surprised you did not pursue him.

Morris: When I first found out that they continued to produce Morris Mios, I was furious. I had seen countless lives lost due to it, all lives that I was unable to save. It was a monstrous concoction.

DI: Sounds like a strong motive for your brother's murder.

Morris: The only thing I could think of at the time was

stopping that production. Finding Nathaniel's killer wasn't my first priority anymore, I had to stop that weapon from getting out.

DI: You left Io Technologies not long after the leak. Why?

Morris: I was lucky to get away with being there for so many years. A note was left on my desk one morning, a week or two after the first headline appeared. It had my real name written on it and a time and place for a meeting. I knew from that it was over. I left immediately.

DI: You didn't go to the meeting?

Morris: No.

DI: So, after leaving Io Technologies, what happened next? Did you continue to pursue Argus?

...

August 2003

Thirteen years pass.

Joseph lives comfortably in a small town north of Corbeck, amongst the mountains. He has a lot of money left over from his years at Io Technologies. He has used some of it to run a small, informal practice to help locals. He only advises, it is harder to fake an identity nowadays.

Although he continues to hunt for his brother's murderer, he is still not totally sure if it could be Argus. That man is still his only lead, but he has vanished. The search becomes half-hearted as he grows comfortable within the small town. He finds that the tormenting memories of the war and his past life are distant here.

He has made his home in a cabin, on the outskirts of the town. The Magnus is wilder up in the mountains, it roils and cascades towards the valley. It makes Joseph realise how lucky he was to survive it all those years ago. If he had fallen in at this point, he would not have awoken at the other end.

The clearing in which is home stands is populated by shamrocks. They create a green carpet that lead to his front door. Inside there are only two rooms, a living room with kitchenette and a separate bedroom that is also home to the bathroom. The wooden floors are dressed in rugs and scenic paintings hang on the walls. Joseph believes he has found his peace.

But there are boxes in the corners, overflowing with papers and notes. His hunt for Argus has certainly diminished, he reflects. The papers are taken out and reviewed less and less these days.

Again, he leaves them where they are, choosing instead to make the small journey into town. He is approaching the turning point that will be his half century on this Earth. He feels content however, and ready to welcome it.

As he approaches the town's main road, he sees a Marbled White butterfly perched on the flower of a lilac wisteria. Its black wings are speckled with white, and he wonders whether it is a bad omen or a good one. It flutters about him and seemingly follows him along the street.

Peacefully, he enjoys watching it flicker left and right, as if catching air currents that he cannot feel. It briefly lands on the glass front of the newsagents, and he realises it was an omen after all. Staring at him from the black and white print of the paper was his niece.

He rushes into the store, practically throwing his change at the clerk as he grabs a copy. Back on the street, he sits on the curb, hungrily devouring the news of his family. Anna has been married for several years (he had missed so much!) and was celebrating the birth of her first son. But the birth was tainted with sadness, the article was an obituary for her late husband, Harrison.

The paper is burning between his fingertips and it is in flames before he realises. He remains on the curb amongst the ashes as he considers what to do. What world was this little boy going to grow up into? Would his family history follow him?

Before he has a chance to rethink, to consider the potential danger he is putting himself in, Joseph has hurried back to his temporary home and clambered into his battered truck. Now he is driving south, towards Corbeck. He is speeding, and he winces each time the suspension clatters when hitting a pothole in the road.

The familiarity of the town sends shivers racing through his veins. He finds his heart rate increases whenever he sees something tainted by memory; the church where his brother got married, the park they used to play in together as children, the bench they used to sit on and share ice-cream with their father.

He avoids the police station like vermin avoid the broom. Instead, he heads for the hospital. It is different to how he remembers. He trained here, treated his first patients before he was called to war. The surroundings still evoke a sense of hope in him, the potential for lives to be saved.

He is calm as he asks the receptionist about his niece. She informs him that Anna had left early that morning and that she and baby was doing well. He claims to be a private doctor, from a town downriver, brought in to help her through such a vulnerable and difficult time.

"But I was told she would still be here? And I have not been given an address,"

The receptionist is happy to help him, she is worried for the skinny, gaunt woman who had left alone that morning with a newborn. Joseph thanks her profusely and leaves, his nerves sparking in anticipation of seeing his niece again after so many years.

He sees her from across the road. She is sitting on a wicker chair on her veranda, a bundle of cloths clutched to her breast. The baby. A tuft of dark hair can be seen sprouting from the bundle. She is staring into space. The effort of staying strong in light of her husband's death and child's birth has drawn her face tight, her features are haggard and tired.

The baby's sudden cry causes her to flinch, and she catches sight of the stranger staring at her from across the road. There is no flicker of recognition, no warmth of familiarity. She shows only fear as she gropes for her things and hurries inside.

There is nothing he can do, Joseph realises. The woman holding a child is not the niece he remembers, the face that was round and always flushed with joy. He scolds himself for his stupidity. He is uncertain as to what he truly expected, but her running in fear was not one of them.

Instead of knocking on the door that was, he had no doubt, now firmly locked, he simply leaves. As he begins the long drive back to his own town, he takes stock of the situation. He has plenty of money left from his days at Io Technologies, hidden away in various banks slowly gaining interest. The least he can do is provide for her, having abandoned her for so long.

However, before reaching the outskirts of Corbeck, he is suddenly drawn away from the main road. Steering with trembling hands, he takes the turning for the Morris estate, and trundles up towards his old home.

It looks as exactly as it had all those years ago. As he stands at the gates, he sees his younger self. He stands in a tattered, worn uniform and he is so relieved to be home after so many difficult years. He foolishly believed that he will be able to leave the war behind him.

Joseph does not feel relief now, but anxious anticipation. He rings an automated buzzer, a new addition, and requests a meeting with Edith Morris. The gruff voice on the other end demands to know who he is, but Joseph only responds with "I'm family, she'll know me when she sees me,"

Begrudgingly, he is allowed through the gates. The gravel crunches gratingly beneath his feet and he nervously rubs his palms together, despite the heat emanating from them. He is made to wait for some time on the doorstep, long enough that he begins to wonder if he has been forgotten about. It gives him time to question why he is here, what he thought he could possibly gain by talking to Edith. Maybe some information? An apology? He laughs scornfully at his own naivety.

When the door suddenly swings open, Joseph's fear forces his heart to falter. Argus' expression reflects Joseph's shock, his eyes wide behind his glasses. In that single, frozen moment, Joseph realises the true murderer of his brother.

CHAPTER 5
26/11/2019

DI: Do you know why Argus was present at the Morris household on that day?

Morris: I do not. Rumour had it he was searching for people like himself.

DI: Like Poppy Dunkeany?

Morris: Yes.

DI: Mr Morris, at the beginning of this interview, you said that you felt you could not return because no one would have listened to you. Are you aware there was a testimony that would have supported you in trial?

Morris: At the time, no. But I am aware of this now, yes.

DI: Margaret's statement was taken two days after the event. She was only four years old. She has since succumbed to mental illness which means, as of the time this interview has been taken, she is unable to provide another reliable testimony. But her first is thought to still carry some weight in court. The evidence needed to overturn this testimony would have been a signed confession from the guilty party.

Morris: I know.

DI: When did you learn of this testimony?

...

May 2010

The beach meets the ocean amicably. The waves roll across its surface for a long distance, lethargically stretching out to the dunes pitted with marram grass. Cliffs tower at either end, sheltering the bay from the harsher sea winds. The gulls, usually loud and boisterous, settle contentedly in their inaccessible cliff nests.

A young girl plays alone on the wide expanse of beach. She delves her hands deeply into the sand, letting it trickle between her childish fingers as the coastal breeze whips fair hairs around her head. She begins pulling and pushing the sand into shapes, forming and building a fortress. Occasionally she commits to the long trek to the ocean, fills a red plastic bucket with seawater, and trudges back, carefully holding it so as not to spill any.

A woman, her mother, sits nearby on a plaid blanket. Her bare legs stretch out, toes buried in the sand, sunglasses shielding her face from the sun. She feels calm, serene almost. The constant murmur of the waves lapsing onto the beach lulls her into a doze. The book she has been reading has fallen from between her fingers.

A sudden commotion brutally pulls her from her reverie. Her daughter is angrily stomping across her creation. Her cheeks flush, she is shouting to herself, furiously swiping at the sand with her hands. The mother hurriedly clambers to her feet, running to her child.

On reaching her, she grabs her by the wrists and looked deeply into the child's eyes. The child avoids her gaze, scowling down at the pile of sand.

"Bella, why are you destroying Bee's castle?" the mother asks her.

"It's rubbish!" she responds savagely.

"I thought it looked very good,"

"No!" the child argues, "It was bad. It had no turrets! She wouldn't let me add turrets!"

The girl's face wavers for a moment, briefly losing her defiant expression. There seems to be an internal struggle before the girl's voice bursts forth again, "I don't want turrets!"

The mother sighs, "Bee, why don't you want Bella to add turrets?"

The girl's lip trembles as she maintains eye contact and she murmurs something quietly.

"I didn't catch that Bee,"

The girl is now wringing her hands, ashamedly looking at the piled sand at her feet, "She doesn't make pretty ones,"

"Maybe you can help her make pretty ones? By guiding like I taught you," the mother suggests, "Would you like that, Bella?"

The girls face shivers again as Bella replaces Bee. Her brow gains a stubborn edge and her jaw clenches, "Sandcastles are hard, I want to go crab fishing,"

The girl's face suddenly lights up as an idea hits her like a flash of lightening, "We could make a castle for the crabs!" Bee announces.

The girl grins, "I'd like that,"

The mother smiles, happy that her daughters are once again playing together. She strolls languidly back to her blanket, managing to push her worries away for the time being. Arabella would learn, she decides. It had been a shock at first, to learn that she actually had two children instead of one. Their father had been unable to cope. But both Bella and Bee were growing into two beautiful and independent young girls who were gradually learning to coexist in a single body.

Arabella's ability of personality dimorphism could be a blessing yet.

As she settles herself again on the blanket, the mother lightly dusts sand from the cloth. She distractedly begins to watch figures stroll along the sea front. One in particular catches her attention, for he is heading towards her.

She gazes steadfastly towards the thread that joins the sky to the sea, hoping he is not coming for her. However, she could no longer ignore the stranger when he stops a few feet away from her.

"Margaret?" she barely recognises his voice.

"Who are you?" she demands harshly.

"It's me. I've searched for a long time to find you,"

Standing there, wearing rumpled clothing and a weathered face, Margaret struggles to link the uncle she knew to the haggard man before her. He reminds her far more of her father, but she had promised herself not to think of him. But that was impossible. Impossible now that this stranger wearing her father's face was speaking to her.

"Please leave," the words escape her in an exhale of air.

"I'm sorry?"

"You need to go," she says more firmly, "I don't want you here, go away!"

"Margaret, I want to help you. You and your daughter,"

Silently, they take a moment to watch the child as she digs through rock pools, searching for crabs.

"How can you help me?" she asks, her words a whisper. Here they are, the unwanted, trickster memories, bubbling up. She had done so well to contain them, but they are welling up once more, ready to deceive her once again.

"You murdered him," She could hear the noise, the final crack, echoing across the chasm of the years. It was hidden in the sounds of the waves slapping against the sand, the clatter of pebbles against rocks thrown by her child. The audible snapping of her father's life being snatched away.

Despondency is clear in his features; she sees it lining his eyes and the downwards curve of his mouth. That was not the face. Not the face that hovered behind her father's dying mask.

She points accusingly at him, her finger trembling as she attempts to sort through the contradicting memories, "It wasn't you, but I was told it was!"

Hours of therapy. Hours upon hours of being told her memory was wrong, that she was mistaken, that she had seen her uncle.

"I saw it happen," she whines reproachfully, "And it wasn't you,"

CHAPTER 6
26/11/2019

DI: In the past forty years, you returned to Corbeck twice. This is the third time. What made you return again?

Morris: I discovered evidence of which I thought could be used to finally clear my name.

DI: Ah, the contract. You have submitted it as a vital piece of evidence in the case against
Io Technologies, initiated by Mrs Anna Lee?

Morris: Yes.

DI: Where did you find this evidence?

...

December 2014

The lock is supposed to be an easy one. In reality, his hands are trembling to such an extent that it has morphed into one of great difficulty. His desperation is outweighing his caution, the possibility of being this close to locating evidence is too much. Joseph is sure he knows what happened to his brother, but he had to be able to prove it.

Finally, the lock announces its surrender with a satisfying click. The door swings inwards, revealing Argus' office, a room he had spent so many years searching for. It is... small. He had expected a wide expanse of a room, floor to ceiling bookshelves, an expensive mahogany desk.

Instead, an Ikea desk squats in the corner and one wall is lined with dull grey filing cabinets. The remaining wall space is hidden behind cardboard boxes, piled six high, spilling over with documents. Joseph shuts the door quietly behind him, it clicks shut, locking once again. He accepts the challenge and systematically begins to search.

As he investigates, flicking through the first filing cabinet, he remembers the faces of all those he had weaned information from to get to this point. The overweight, bulbous jowls of the board of directors of Io Technologies; the emaciated faces of the organisers of the illegal Chikara battles.

He recalls one of them so clearly. A battered man, Johnson, whose eyes were shadowed and sunken from years of drug addiction. He had fought in many Chikara in his youth, a powerful and promising electro-kinaesthetic who foiled his chances when he discovered imps. After years of abuse, he could barely manipulate a charge, never mind arc lightening through the air.

They had met at an underground, abandoned station, the most recent venue for the illegal Chikara battles. That day, the fight had been between two underaged girls and Joseph had stubbornly averted his eyes from the fight, knowing he would be unable to bear the sight if one of them got hurt.

Johnson had been in constant motion, his fingers dancing on his knees as if playing an invisible piano. But Joseph wondered what tune it was playing; his face was pulled tight in a frown, listening uncomfortably to the discordant music of his fingertips that only he could hear.

"I used to be able to do that," he muttered distractedly, twitchily nodding towards the flashes of electricity of one of the players, "I was the best!"

The words came out in a violent spit, and Joseph found it difficult to steer the conversation back, "You said you worked with Argus?"

"End of the 70s yeah, when I was just starting out,"

"I worked with him in the 80s, I've got a really important message for him," Joseph lied, cringing at the poor attempt.

"Yeah?" Johnson's gaze roamed the crowds, he was barely listening to what Joseph had to say anyway.

"You know where he is now?"

"Yeah,"

"Have you got an address?" Joseph pressed.

Johnson's twitches suddenly ceased, and Joseph was unnerved by his unexpected stillness. Johnson's eyes bored into him, seemingly like black holes in the dim light. He was so still; it was like having a staring contest with a cadaver.

"Johnson?"

The noise of the match became muted, as if a bubble had formed around them. Joseph's heart thundered, had he gone too far? Asked too much? He allowed a heat to form in the palms of his hand, ready. But the bubble was shrinking, he could feel the panic expanding in his chest, pushing outwards beyond his body.

Johnson moved so suddenly that Joseph was barely able to disguise his flinch. He launched away, a reanimated creature.

"That's my dealer!" he hissed through his cracked teeth, "Hey!" He shouted across the crowds, desperately forcing his way through. His arms swung in haphazard circles, swimming against the tide of people. Without thinking, Joseph's hand had flung out, catching Johnson's flailing limb in a heated grasp.

"Hey, I need to get to him, let go!" Johnson tugged against the grip, so desperate for the next hit that he barely registered the smoking of his jacket.

Taking advantage of his leverage, Joseph demanded through clenched teeth, "Address, now,"

"I dunno man!" Johnson's spindly fingers scrabbled at Joseph's sleeve, pathetically trying to pull him away, "I need to go,"

"If you tell me, I'll give you the money," he blurted, his mind working overtime to figure out what Johnson wanted most, "I'll give you a hundred," he promised.

Johnson's eyes widened, and Joseph was disgusted by the ugly shine in them, "Serious?"

"Yeah, tell me the address first," he repeated.

"Kalverstatt, in downtown. Pearson Building,"

The crowd jostled him as he dug out a pile of notes and handed them to Johnson. He winced at his own handiwork. He had burned through Johnson's jacket and the shirt underneath, leaving tender red welts on his lower arm. But so frenzied was Johnson, by the sight of his deal and the money as well as the prospect of his next hit, he had not even noticed. He was lost to the crowd in seconds.

That had been several weeks ago. Joseph had found the address easily, developing a routine of surveillance of the street before he even thought about entering the building. Each time he saw Argus, strolling down the street as if he did not have countless felonies shadowing him, Joseph's heart would constrict. As he watched him disappear into the building, Joseph would have to rush to the bathroom, dousing himself in cool water to dampen his angry, flaming hands.

But he is here now, inside. He feels calm, focusing on the task at hand. He has quickly figured Argus' filing system, the filing cabinets only hold documents A-G and so he begins flicking through the cardboard boxes, searching for M.

"Out-dated," he mutters as he rearranges piles of

cardboard boxes to access those in the back corner, "Everything is kept online now Argus, even I know that,"

There are four boxes that could contain what he is looking for. He is now surrounded by boxes, and there is a nagging worry tugging at the back of his mind that he will not be able to remember where they all sat originally. Would Argus even notice, he wonders, how does he keep track of all this?

There it is! A document folder labelled 'Morris Mios'.

He quickly flicks through, excitement causing his fingers to tremble now, opposed to anxiety. He pulls the original contract from the sheath of papers. His excitement is quickly morphing to anger. He glares at the signature at the bottom of the page. It clearly does not belong to his brother.

The entire document is fraudulent.

He looks around at the boxes surrounding him. How many other lives are trapped here? Caught in Argus' spiderweb of fake contracts, lies and deceit?

"I need to burn it," he whispers. All his life, he had been cautious. He knew all too well how fire could spread, how quickly it became uncontrollable. He feels a flitter of excitement at the prospect of freely burning this place to the ground. All this paper, it is so easy for it to catch alight.

He shoves the entire folder under his coat, already feeling his hands beginning to warm. But there is a sound outside the corridor. Footsteps. Footsteps that are growing louder for each second he stands frozen. The room is so bare, there is nowhere to hide.

Unless?

Joseph crouches in the corner, haphazardly building the cardboard boxes into a fortress. He crouches, panicked, the cool side of a filing cabinet pressed against his shoulder. He must rely on the desperate hope that Argus would not notice the displaced boxes.

He hears the scratching of the key in the lock and clamps his hands to his mouth, smothering the sound of his own breathing. There is only a slither of space between the boxes he is hiding behind, and it only affords a limited view. But he clearly hears multiple people enter the room.

"Are you truly able to do this?" a clear, articulate voice demands. He recognises it immediately, and shivers erupt down his spine. His heart contracts as ice cold dread washes over him.

"I only want one gone," the voice continues.

Argus strolls casually into view, waving his hand dismissively, "Yes, yes, I can do this,"

Joseph can now see Edith, who is viciously gripping onto something just out of his sight, "Her ability is simply becoming a nuisance now, I thought I could harness it into something else, but she is being particularly difficult!"

This final word is paired with a savage tug, and Arabella is pulled into view. Her warm, blonde hair is plaited, and one school sock has sunk to her ankle. Chewing a nail anxiously, she seems to be having an argument with herself. Joseph did not understand his great niece's ability, he could not comprehend the concept of two people coexisting in the same mind. Whether he understood it or not, however, it was Arabella's ability. It was what made her special. Edith was talking as if it could be taken away.

Argus kneels before Arabella, speaking gently, "Who am I speaking with?" he asks.

"Bee," Arabella responds quietly. Her brow is furrowed in worry, and she has bitten her nail clean off. Blood is swelling from the quick.

"Do you understand what's happening Bee?"

"You're trying to take me away!" she spits fiercely.

"Ah, so you must be Bella," Argus smiles, "We're not going to take you away Bella, we're just fixing the balance,"

"The balance is fine!" Bella begins, but she shivers and stutters mid-sentence, interrupted by Bee, "What do you mean, balance?"

"Your balance is off. Bella is taking too much control.

If we don't do something now, there may be no Bee left,"

Arabella considers Argus, her face a storm of emotions. She is tormented. Her eyes erratically glance around the room and she seems unable to stop gnawing on her thumb.

Edith attempts an encouraging smile, but to Joseph it is the smile of a wolf's snarl, "We just want to help you, Bee. You're my good little girl, aren't you? So, stay in charge, for your Granny,"

Joseph realises he needs to interject. He should leap out from his hiding place, fists blazing, and sweep this child away from the inevitable danger. But he does not move. Instead, he continues watching as the events unfold.

Arabella seems to come to a decision. The anger in her face melts away as she holds Edith's gaze, "Okay Granny,"

Granny is supposed to protect the little girl from the wolf, not lead her to his lair.

Argus gently presses his fingertips to Arabella's temple. She frowns uncomfortably, clenching her fists in determination. But suddenly, there is a shift, a change in her demeanour that Joseph does not quite catch, and she is thrashing and screaming wildly.

"Don't take me away!" she shrieks, her fingers curling into claws as she scratched at Argus, "Leave me alone!"

"Bee! Come on now, you cannot let her take over!" Edith scolds, taking her granddaughter by the shoulders. Her voice drops as she speaks, developing into a soothing tone, "You are stronger than her Bee. We are not taking her away,"

Arabella is shaking her head, tears bursting, "This is wrong! This is wrong! You said you wouldn't take her away," she cries, "Leave me alone! Please, don't!"

There is one final, fearful cry and then an awful ripping sound. Joseph cannot bear to look, he hides his face in his hands, shame filling each pore of his body. It is dragging him down, pulling him to the cheap carpeted floor. It takes a moment before he is able to lift his head again.

She is touching her face, fingertips rapidly dancing

across her skin, "Where are you? Bella, where have you gone?"

The yawning emptiness stuns Bee. The void that has replaced her sister is all encompassing and suffocating. She is teetering on the edge. As she pushes trembling hands through her hair, erratically tugging it into knots, she feels herself falling into the vast chasm. The delicate balance between her sister and herself has been infinitely thrown off, and Bee loses herself in the sudden space.

Joseph only watches. The acidic taste of bile rises to his throat in response to the horrifying scene and his own inability to stop it. Each muscle is clenched, every nerve firing warning alarms. His body is braced for fight or flight. But he is frozen.

Argus gently passes a mask to Edith. An exact replica of Arabella's face. But not. Joseph sees it now; he sees the clear differences that were hidden to him before.

"This is it?" Edith stares dumbly at the small mask in the palms of her hand.

"That's her Essence, yes," Argus confirms with an irritated sigh, "Are we done?"

"Yes," Edith response is a whisper as she gently traces a finger around the mask. She pulls a handkerchief from her shoulder back and wraps it carefully around it. She handles it gingerly, uncertain of its structure. How could something solid and inanimate like this be formed from her granddaughter?

Argus ushers them out of the office. Bee's expression is one of complete bewilderment, she seems unable to tether herself to the reality around her. She follows her grandmother dreamily, barely registering the slamming of the door behind them.

Resting his forehead against its surface, Argus swears beneath his breath. His shoulders have slumped, and beads of perspiration have gathered on his forehead. He rubs his eyes, pushing his glasses up with his knuckles.

"I don't think I did that right," he mutters.

ESSENCE

He leaves shortly after. Joseph feels exhaustion snake into his limbs, but he knows that there is one thing he needs to do before he leaves. He allows some time before emerging from his hiding place. He is nauseous, bile swirls in his stomach. He pushes the feeling away as he presses his palms firmly against the nearest cardboard box.

...

DI: I remember that fire. It took six fire engines to control the blaze.

Morris: I did what I believed to be right.

DI: Was it right to destroy an entire city block?

Morris: ...

DI: Let's move on. Mr Morris, we are also under the understanding that there is a signed confession to the murder of Nathaniel in existence. Do you know of this?

Morris: ...

DI: Mr Morris?

Morris: Yes.

DI: Did you sign it?

Morris: Yes

DI: Of your own volition or were you under duress?

Morris: Under duress.

DI: Do you know where this confession is?

Morris: What?

DI: After searching the Morris estate we have yet been unable to add this confession to the evidence as it has not been located. I think we'll leave it there.

Part 3

Chikara

CHAPTER 1
16th January 2013

There was always a part of Mallory Dunkeany that never settled. From four years old, ever since her ability developed far earlier than her peers, she felt a constant anticipation, always jittery with nerves. Her mind was erratic, she had to work hard to train her attention otherwise her focus would slip like water leaking from a cracked pipe. Important facts would fail to stay in her head, whilst useless information like Chikara stats would lodge themselves permanently.

When she complained about it at nine years old, her ability had been haphazardly blamed. That was the time that Poppy was diagnosed as powerless. The fact that Mallory could be unhappy with such a gift became a difficult topic of conversation. So, she suffered quietly.

It was like the constant buzzing of a telephone left of its hook. Her power was searching for an outlet, there was too much of it flowing through her. She needed someone, something, to lift her back onto the cradle and stop the endless white noise.

But this. Here.

This was that something.

Chikara.

The girl moves in fluid motions, her arms languidly circling the ball of water, hands poised. Her fingers arch and a small burbling bubble of liquid is pulled away from the central orb. Gracefully, she flicks a wrist. The water arcs, crossing the space between the fighters in seconds and landing in the opponent's eye. He flinches, blinks, momentarily disorientated. His rising attack is muted as he wipes the water from his face.

She pauses, the flow of water momentarily dammed as her opponent lunges forwards. But even Mallory can see that he has misjudged his step, his foot skidding a fraction too far. There is a second where his attack is ugly and forced, surging forwards unevenly. The girl leaps on the advantage, releasing her dam. The water breaks against his face, the sound like a wave on wet sand. It rolls up, cresting his lips and nostrils until he is spluttering and retching on his knees.

He concedes, walks away from the ring, still coughing as if he had swallowed gallons of water opposed to the contents of a water bottle.

Mallory is barely able to breathe, her lungs contracting in excitement. Her ability senses the display of powers before her, and for the first time in years it softens the buzzing. She can actually think clearly, her focus crystal sharp as she follows the flowing movement of bodies. She has found it. She's meant to be part of this.

Moments later, a second opponent is stepping into the ring. Or, more accurately, stomping. Mallory is sure she feels the ground shake beneath her. His muscles bulge grotesquely from his short sleeves. Each breath tests the endurance of the material as his muscled chest rises and falls. She quickly establishes this new opponent to be Mesomorphic, despite a lack of introduction. Mesomorphs have the ability to heal muscle damage extraordinarily quickly, allowing the exponential growth of muscle mass. The lawlessness and illegality of Chikara dictated quick, continuous matches. There is no time for breaks, introductions, or winning announcements. At any point, they could run out of time.

The giant lunges forward. There is no skill to his movement, no strategy to his train-like momentum. There is simply the draw of the enemy. Abilities have a heavy influence on one's prospects. Mallory knows she will be expected to pursue an electrician's career, like how her father, a Magnetism Kinaesthetic, pursued a career with metals. How ability suppressors tended towards teachers. But there is no career a Mesomorphic is inclined to. They are bred to be brutish.

The girl easily side steps the attack, she seems to ripple from one space to another. She has hurriedly gathered more water, and it undulates between the palms of her hands as she studies her opponent. He is struggling to fix on her, the ever-moving target is confusing him. He leaps clumsily sideways, in an attempt to predict where she will appear. He fails. His arms swipes at the air and the lack of resistance throws him off balance.

The girl again takes the advantage, darting behind the beast and dropping her globe of liquid at his feet. Mallory watches in awe as the girl leaps onto her opponents back, placing her fingers firmly to his temples.

The signs of dehydration are immediate. As the girl draws the liquid from the surface of his skin, the Mesomorph's skin begins to dry, his lips cracking. He bellows, grabbing her collar and throwing her over his shoulders. At the unexpected grip, the girl gasps, releasing all the gathered water. Her grip breaks as the water splatters across him, and she tumbles to the concrete in a tangle of limbs.

His breath is heavy. The water trickles down the side of his face as he licks cracked lips with a sandpapery tongue. He stands in a puddle of water. Water that should be flowing internally rather than stagnating at his feet.

The girl is still on the ground. Mallory can see her arm is bent at the wrong angle, that the pain is sparking through

ESSENCE

her and preventing her from clambering to her feet. Mallory does not want to see her lose, especially to a grunt like this who got a lucky throw in.

The water has trickled across the paving slabs, beginning to pool at her own school shoes. It triggers the idea and she does not hesitate. She crouches, gathering the excess buzzing from her veins into the palm of her hand. It crackles and she lets it take the route of least resistance. The small trickle of water that leads to the Mesomorph's feet.

The entire crowd is confused by the sudden convulsions. The inexplicable collapse of their favourite. The girl wins by default. She pockets the unexpected winnings, abandoning the scene before anyone can question what had truly occurred. It was viewed as poor sportsmanship to get help from someone in the crowd, and poor sportsmanship was not taken kindly to.

Mallory hurries away, astounded by her own recklessness. She hears the girl calling to her, but she stubbornly ignores it. She is giddy from the fight, from the small part she played in it, the blissful peace following the release of so much energy. But her hands shake with fear as well as adrenaline, with the fear of getting caught, of having witnessed something so incredibly illegal.

She can no longer ignore the calls when the girl grabs her roughly by the shoulder, "Hey! Why are you ignoring me?"

She only gapes as the girl glares at her. Her eyes are inevitably drawn to the ugly brokenness of the girl's arm, the way it is bending unnaturally.

"Uh, shouldn't you go to hospital?" she manages at last.

There is sweat beading on the girl's forehead, but she maintains the rough hold on Mallory's collar, "Not until you tell me why you interfered,"

Mallory was unsure of the answer to that herself. Why had she got involved? It was because of that relentless buzzing, she realised, all that excess energy and suddenly there was an outlet for it and how could she resist?

"I don't know," she lifted her shoulder in a half shrug, her eyes drawn again to the girl's arm, "Seriously though, I think you need to get that looked at,"

For the first time, the girls seems to realise the state of her left arm, "Walk with me," she orders, "And don't think about running off or I'll drain every last bit of moisture out of you,"

There is a real threat behind those words, she easily senses it. The girl had just drained a man that was at least three times her size, but Mallory's mouth is already moving, "Not if I don't shock you first,"

"Real firecracker you, huh? What's your name kid?"

"Mal,"

"I'm Cat, now answer my question,"

Mallory stares at her feet as they cross the cracks in the pavement and shrugs again, "I don't know, I just have this constant buzzing in me, like my ability is in constant overdrive all the time and I guess there was a part of me that wanted to see how far it could go,"

"It went far enough to bring down a Mesomorph, that enough?"

Mallory pauses for a moment, thinking. The buzzing in her veins is already building up again, pulsing through her veins. It had not been enough. She needs more of it.

"No?" Cat laughs incredulously.

"How do you get into this?" she is shocked by her own question. Her? Fighting in Chikara?

Cat shared her disbelief, "Absolutely not. You're just a kid, with way too much energy. You'll grow out of it,"

"I don't think you understand how much energy I have," Mallory's words emerged in a rush of desperation. Her ability has been like this since she was four years old. If she was going to grow out of it, she would have done it by now.

Despite the countless reservations surging through her mind at that moment, she knows above all of it that she had to do this. She had always been like this, constantly unable to rest because there was too much inside her. Now there is a chance for her to release some of the pent-up electricity.

And she knew she'd be good at it.

"Prove it then," Cat places her good hand on her hip. Her other arm hangs limply at her side. How was she not delirious with pain right now?

Mallory glances around. They are stood at a crossing, a busy intersection laid out before them. There are countless traffic lights dotted about, and she can sense the flow of electricity to each bulb. She places her hand on the pedestrian button, but instead of pressing it, she reaches out to the flow.

The intersection lights up. She can see each hair-thin wire, each transformer, each miniscule LED light. She sees the maze, a blueprint hidden beneath the concrete. She connects to the flow, adding every last ounce of energy from her veins into the system.

The result is blinding.

For only a smattering of seconds, the entire road is blind. The traffic lights glow so bright, that they create a false aurora of red, orange and green that reflects off the bumpers of cars and the windows of the buildings lining the road.

Just as quickly, the lights vanish as each traffic light, lamp post and exposed bulb blow. The intersection is plunged into chaos. Driver's horns sound over the crunching of glass from burst lights. Cat stares gobsmacked, a limp hand still shielding her brow.

"You're not on Imps are you?" she demanded.

"Imps?" Mallory had never heard the term.

Cat shakes her head in wonderment, "We have a lot to talk about,"

CHAPTER 2
22nd July 2011

The television screen is a whirl of colours. Athletes whisk in various directions, contorting their bodies in unexpected shapes. Belches of flames are interceded with spouts of water and hissing steam. The two young boys sit before the screen, their eyes unwavering from the action. A bell shrills from the speakers and the boys groan, roll their eyes as a referee storms into the arena.

"Boo!" Mikey spits, "Why's he getting involved?"

There are limits to the organised Chikara battles, countless rules to prevent major injuries. The action is often quick and violent, it rarely lasts more than twenty seconds, but to these boys those seconds are glorious. There is constant interference from the referees, constant interruptions to prevent particularly dangerous abilities from being excessively used.

The boys are unaware of this, however. They simply see the referees as spoil sports.

"He did that, like, ten seconds ago," Aaron agrees grumpily. His grandmother watches over the two boys. She is watching them whilst her son is out with his wife, visiting a therapist for their daughter. She shakes her head at the situation. Powerless.

It shouldn't be. It couldn't be. Their blood was surely too strong.

The action begins again on the television, drawing in the attention of the boys. They shout along with the players; two teams of four battling it out. Today they are in a simple arena, later they will be in a wilder, more extensive battle ground. Those fights are Aaron's favourite. He likes how many of the athletes employ their environment to help them win the battle.

Again, the action lasts mere seconds, but when the fight is stopped, more than just the referee rushes into the arena. Several bodies in florescent green jackets rush to a stricken body in the centre of the floor. To Aaron, it's not obvious at first that the player is hurt. He's confused by the ragdoll at the centre of the screen. It's not until the cameras cut away to grim, pale faces in a studio that he begins to grasp the seriousness of what has just occurred.

"What's happened?" Mikey begins to shout, but Aaron hurriedly shushes him.

"The fight is temporarily suspended as medics-" the formal voice is cut off as the screen turns blank. Aaron and Mikey are left staring at their own reflections.

"Hey!"

"I think that's enough of that," Agatha interrupts brusquely.

"Why did they stop the fight?" Mikey has still not grasped the gravity of the situation. The image of that player laying splayed is fixed in Aaron's mind.

"Someone got hurt," he gulped.

"That happens sometimes," Agatha is buried beneath a blanket, a half-finished cross word on her lap, "Chikara is dangerous, our abilities are dangerous. We have to learn to control and manage them so that we don't hurt one another," she explained.

"Have you ever hurt anyone Gran?"

"Not intentionally," Agatha laughs, but she quickly becomes serious, "It's important that you understand some abilities are stronger than others, as well. And for those who don't have powers, well we need to look after them,"

"Like Poppy?"

"Like Poppy,"

"What's the most dangerous ability?" Mikey asks inquisitively.

Agatha chews her lip in thought, "I don't know dear,"

"Why not?"

"I'm challenging you!" Mikey interrupted, clambering onto to the sofa beside Agatha, "I'm gonna beat you," he announces. He leaps from the sofa, a cushion raised high in his hands. He gives himself a small boost of air current so that he lands on Aaron from a greater height. The boys tussle and Aaron creates a bubble of sounds that sends Mikey abruptly into the air. He lands bewildered on the sofa.

"How did you do that?" he demands, rubbing the sore point on his stomach where the force had connected.

Aaron shrugged, just as confused, "I have no idea, I didn't think you'd fly that far,"

"You need to be careful Aaron," Agatha interrupts. Around her crossword square are shadow drawings of banshees, "Your ability is stronger than others,"

"How'd you mean?"

"You've got a different kind of blood in you, one that intensifies your abilities. You need to be more careful than most,"

"Yes Gran," Aaron nods. Her warning, and the ragdoll body of the Chikara player is already drifting from his mind. But it returns to him that night, and countless nights afterwards. He will become obsessed, searching for the most dangerous abilities. The dreams morph, the injured body becomes family members, his sister, his twin. He begins to practice, readying himself to fight the most dangerous of all abilities. Organic kinaesthetic.

CHAPTER 3
16th October 2019

Mallory liked to believe she was an independent young woman. She was intelligent, practical and above all else, mature. She studied hard, maintained high grades, saved a hefty chunk of each monthly pay cheque from her part time job. Yet she still found herself on the darker streets of Corbeck, marching along to the same rendezvous as she had for the past four years.

Imperium.

Perhaps she was not as independent as she liked to think. Did dependence on drugs count? She could already sense the flutter in her stomach, anticipation for the inevitable surge of power. Her footsteps quickened against the cracked pavement. Even now she struggled to control her excitement.

Imps.

She had never intended to start taking it. Her twelve-year-old self would be appalled. So would the rest of her family. But she was unable to drag herself away. She wasn't addicted to the drugs; she simply loved the feeling. The overwhelming surge of power through her veins, the ease that came with it, of focusing on countless miniscule electrons and manipulating them to do her will.

There was a difference, right?

She paused at the opening of the alley. Was it this one?

You would assume Mallory would know the path to her monthly rendezvous, but her memory was getting worse. Her memory had been poor enough to begin with. It was possibly a result of frazzling her brain once too many times, or maybe her reliance on Imps. Or all those beatdowns she had experienced. She had countless sticky notes scrawled with reminders as well as planners brimming with endless to-do lists. But they were not always Mallory-proof.

Hence why she was running late. She had to return to the changing rooms after netball practice earlier that evening, searching for her bag of school clothes. The session had finished about twenty minutes prior, and the rooms were deserted. As she flicked the lights on, she felt the comfortable buzzing in her veins as the electricity raced through the circuits. Despite the effects of her latest dose of Imps beginning to wear off (they barely lasted a week now) she could still feel the excitement of each and every electron.

It did not take her long to find the bag. It was exactly where she had left it twenty minutes ago when she had stood up and sauntered away without it. It was slumped alone in the corner, and she quickly grabbed it and rushed out, hoping she would manage to catch the next bus. She did not want to be late. This had been a massive waste of her time.

As she left, she flicked the lights off. But the electrical buzzing did not leave her completely. She glanced around the hallway as the evening sunlight flooded in, but all the lights were turned off. There was a set of stairs at the far end of the corridor, and she was just able to make out the glowing light of a single bulb. That explained the persistent buzzing at the base of her skull. She had quickly grown used to the numbing background noise of appliances in the kitchen when her ability had first developed, but the high, uncomfortable frequency of lights-left-on did have a tendency to put her teeth on edge.

The bulb was located in Naomi's office. Her netball coach was notorious for leaving rooms with the lights still on and radios blaring. Mallory resorted to simply jogging up the stairs and flicking it off. She could already hear the radio from the base of the stairs, a heavy bass line sprinkled with the occasional harmony.

But a few steps from the top she heard voices over the music. She knew she was in the wrong and was about to bound back down the stairs when a particular name snagged her attention.

"Ms Morris,"

It was Naomi speaking. Mallory could barely believe it, was it possible Naomi was talking to Travis' grandmother?

She sounded flustered, which was unusual. Mallory stretched forwards, keeping low so as not to be seen through the window in the office door. She held her breath, taking ridiculous care to silently settle into a more comfortable position. Naomi had the ability to hear the slightest noise, or sarcastic comment, from some distance. Mallory could only hope that the radio's noise had drowned out her footsteps.

"I don't know what to say," Naomi continued speaking, "I don't see how I can be of help to you,"

"I understand, Miss Matthews, that you are gifted with an extraordinary ability to not only hear things perfectly from a great distance, but to also differentiate between multiple conversations at once," the voice that spoke was strong but plummy. Mallory suspected the honeyed tones disguised a voice accustomed to receiving exactly what it demanded.

Naomi stuttered, "Well I... uh, I suppose so," Mallory could practically see the blood rising in Naomi's neck as it always did when she was flattered.

"I have heard my brother-in-law is back within the city limits," the voice said, "I am hiring several people whose abilities I have deemed crucial in tracking him down. You are one of those people. I need you to listen out for any talk or gossip regarding him or anything that may possibly relate to him,"

Mallory held a hand to her mouth, amazed at what she was hearing. This was an unbelievable coincidence. As if they had only been talking about this family a week ago at dinner! She resolved to tell her siblings as soon as possible. Of course, she would also have to warn them about the brother-in-law. She would have to find a method of persuasion that stopped them leaving the house at night.

As these thoughts raced around her head, Mallory neglected to notice her water bottle working its way free of the confines of her bag. As a result, when it finally launched itself from her bag, she was far too slow to catch it as it clattered down the steps.

She swore, frozen briefly in indecision as the voices halted suddenly. The noise of the radio wavered then ceased.

"Who's there?" Naomi called.

She bolted, flying down the stairs and through the doors into the cool October air before Naomi had even left her seat and opened the office door to check the corridor. Even now, as she took another turn down the backstreets of the town, she was unsure whether she had gotten away with her eavesdropping. Unlikely, since she definitely didn't have that bag of school clothes with her. She desperately hope she had left them on the bus and not on the steps outside of Naomi's office.

But that wasn't something she needed to be worrying about right now. She was moments away from her next Imps dose. She practically skipped to a stop at the sight of an old friend, Catherine Blumére.

Cat was a few years older than Mallory, an Aqueous Kinaesthetic. She had been one of the Chikara battlers all those years ago; Mallory had been in awe at the ease of her movements, the way she flowed between the attacks of her opponent, striking viciously at every opportunity.

It was Cat who had entered Mallory in her first illegal Chikara.

This evening she was tucked comfortably into a leather jacket, a strip of recent blue dye rejuvenating in her hair. Mallory tugged awkwardly at her braid, sheepishly pulling her coat tighter to hide her netball uniform. Even now, all these years later, she was entranced by Cat's effortless, cool look. That had been her too, not so long ago.

"How many this month Mal?" Cat asked, disregarding small talk. There was a hint of sadness to her question.

"An extra couple on top of the usual," Mallory stubbornly ignored the Cat's expression of disappointment. Cat dug into her bag, glancing over her shoulder as she did so.

"How much do I owe you?"

"These ones are on the house,"

She stares at her in disbelief.

"If you come back,"

"No Cat,"

"Our teams gone down the drain since you left, we've losing every fight. We'll never be able to go pro without you. You were our best,"

"How much do I owe you," Mallory repeated through gritted teeth.

"Mal-"

"Cat, you know why I quit. I couldn't handle it anymore, you think I could stand in a fight now? I can't even get through the week without this," she responds, ripping open the packet with trembling fingers, "How the hell do you think I'd go pro? Imagine the test results, the scandal,"

"That's not true Mal, you're just as powerful without it,"

Mallory stubbornly shakes her head, viciously chewing the tablet into a fine dust. It tasted sweet as it coated the back of her throat. Already, her senses were heightening. She could sense the sparks of electricity in each nerve of Cat's body.

"You think I could do this without Imps?" She demanded, her temper welling in her chest. At the snap of her fingers, every bulb within two hundred meters burst. The violent pop and flash of light was followed by the soft tinkling of glass as the two girls were plunged into darkness.

To Mallory's surprise, her old friend burst into laughter. The sound echoed off the brick walls, grating against her eardrums.

"You know what's even funnier Mal?" Cat's eyes narrowed, glistening with fury, "Those aren't even Imps, they're sugar pills. It's fricking sherbet,"

"What?"

"You haven't taken Imps for at least six months," she wiped her eyes as the last breaths of laughter escaped her, "Go buy yourself a pack of refreshers Mal, save yourself the money,"

With that, Cat sauntered away into the darkness. Abandoned, Mallory slumped against the wall, staring bewildered between the packet in her hand and the shattered lightbulbs.

CHAPTER 4
14th September 2019

In Westgate Forest, to the north of the Morris' home, lies the abandoned rail yard. The forest had encroached on the space. The neglected buildings had succumbed to rust and decay, collapsing in on themselves a little more each year. The disused tracks, which lazily wound from the North to the South, were now intertwined with dandelions and cowslips, although these had died back during the winter months.

Aaron picked his way across the mostly hidden tracks, jumping puddles and weaving between carriages. Many of them were graffitied. The colours glowed starkly in the dim, waxing moonlight. They hid the scorch marks, caused nearly forty years ago when the train yard first closed. The glass windows had long been smashed, and the carriages were now hollow metal coffins trapped to their tracks.

A breeze ruffled the heather and bracken around the wheels of the carriages, and Aaron knew he was getting close.

Benji and Mikey stood in a gravel clearing. The breeze was much stronger here, a gusting wind that whipped loose leaves into a frenzy. Aaron hung back as the air current tugged at his shirt.

"Ready?" Benji called over the wind. Mikey, who's eyes were squeezed shut in concentration, only nodded. Benji placed his hands firmly on Mikey's shoulders and the intensity of the breeze increased.

Mikey brought his hands together, focusing the currents of air. With his fingers splayed and palms facing outwards, he pushed forwards and up, directing the current beneath a carriage. The wind whistled, hooting in excitement as it lifted one side of the carriage.

"Nearly there!" Benji yelled, but his words were whipped away to join the assault on the carriage. It was tipping precariously, but Mikey's arms were beginning to tremble with the effort.

"Come on, come on," Aaron whispered under his breath.

The whistling reached a crescendo before suddenly dying. The carriage slammed back into its place on the tracks, the boom reverberating through the forest.

Aaron applauded as Mikey, with hands on his knees, gasped for breath. He grinned at Aaron, "You see that?" he panted, "Furthest I've ever got,"

"You made a real difference Benj," Aaron commented. Benji nodded shyly, pleased that his effort had been noticed.

"No Travis?" Aaron asked.

Benji shook his head, "Not yet,"

"Maybe he's turning into a part-timer like you, huh?" Mikey joked.

"Very funny," Aaron flicked Mikey's cap off his head, but Mikey caught it with a small breeze, "I've got some news, but I want to wait until Travis gets here,"

"What news is that?"

"A little news about Chikara try outs in the Summer,"

"Have you found out where they're at?" Mikey asked excitedly.

Aaron teasingly tapped his nose, grinning.

"Close?"

"Maybe,"

Despite still gasping for breath, Mikey managed an ecstatic fist pump. Aaron watched as Benji laughed, and he smiled at how the late afternoon sunlight dappled his hair.

"But I'm not telling until Travis gets here," he repeated, shaking the thoughts of Benji from his mind.

Several minutes later, as the boys settled into their routine of drills, a snapping of twigs announced Travis' arrival. He blundered into the clearing, picking loose leaves from his hair.

"Why do we have to practice all the way out here?" he demanded grumpily, shaking his head.

"You know how some of our families would react if they knew what we were doing," Benji reminded him.

"I don't even want to think about it," Mikey made a face, his dark eyes gaining a faraway look as he contemplated his grandmother's likely reaction. He shivered involuntarily.

"Then surely there's an easier way to get here," Travis continued complaining.

"There is, you just always take the wrong turning," rolling his eyes, Aaron pointed to a much wider, clearer track to Travis' left. Travis ignored him, rolling his sleeves up as he prepared for the session.

"Do you want to start now?" Benji asked.

Travis nodded his head decisively, "I want to get going, I'm worried I'm out of practice,"

"You okay to do it on your own?" Benji wiped the sweat from his forehead, "I'm kinda running empty right now,"

"No worries,"

Travis placed his palms flat against the cold metal of the train carriage. His forehead creased as he focused. He concentrated on sending out chromatophores as far as he could reach. He felt them shudder and spread, spiralling away from him into the depths of the material. Once they were spread as far as he could reach, he focused on changing their colour. Navy blue. Forest green. Tones of brown and grey. And black, to mirror the onset of the darkness.

He was transforming the colour of the train to match the forest behind, effectively camouflaging it. He held it for as long as he could, straining to keep the chromatophores spread out and the right colour. But he quickly felt them begin to fizz and jump, losing energy and fading. They sucked on his power, pulling it ravenously from his hands.

Eventually he gasped and let go.

Sweating, he turned to Mikey, "Did I manage it?"

Mikey shrugged, "Sorta,"

Aaron showed Travis a photo of the carriage on his phone. Or, at least, two separate ends of a carriage. The entire centre had seemingly vanished. The camouflage radiated from Travis at its centre. The train shimmered at the edges as it blended into existence again.

"That's really good, it's the furthest you've ever gotten!" Benji said encouragingly.

Travis only sighed frustratedly, exasperated that he couldn't make the entire train disappear.

"Maybe you could try with me supporting," Benji suggested, "That might help,"

"Sure, okay,"

After a few minutes to recover, Travis placed his hands on the cold metal again. This time, as he began to push the chromatophores through the metal, he felt Benji's hands take firm hold of his shoulders. He felt the energy shoot through his veins and out through his fingertips, catapulting the chromatophores further. He surfed on the energy wave, easily manipulating the colours. He was sure this would be it!

Aaron watched in awe as the train seemingly flickered in and out of existence. The camouflage flowered over its surface like a fungus, platelets of colour multiplying outwards in a kaleidoscopic pattern. It was difficult to keep track of them individually, but as a whole the train was disappearing.

He managed to snap a photo before the camouflage collapsed in on itself and Travis stumbled backwards, breathing heavily. He hurried over, unable to contain his glee has he showed an exhausted Travis the photo.

"Completely gone," he announced.

Travis could only grin, unable to get enough breath to say anything.

"So, news on the Chikara trials that I think we are finally ready for!" Aaron beamed, "They are only in the next town over and they start next Spring and I have taken the initiative of signing us up!"

CHAPTER 5
17th October 2019

Mallory shifted uncomfortably in the chair, anxiously straightening her school skirt. Nervous static raced over her skin, the hairs on the nape of her neck standing to attention. She had suspected a conversation would be forthcoming after the night before. Of course she had been heard! But for it to happen so quickly? And like this?

Resting her elbows on the desk, Naomi steepled her fingers into what she believed was a confidential pose. The form that lay between them was a gamble on her part, but from the ashen expression on Mallory's face, Naomi was certain she had bet right.

"Thank you for joining me, Mallory," she began, clearing her desk of the results form. She placed another folder over it, deliberately allowing the name and title to still be readable. Mallory's eyes followed the black and white print as it was offhandedly swept to the side. It couldn't be possible? How had she found out? She had been so careful, and after what Cat had said the previous night, there was no way she could be positive.

Pulling her face into a parody of comfort and

reassurance, Naomi continued, "I know this may seem a little unusual, but I have some concerns, I am…" she paused as she groped for the appropriate term, "I am worried for you,"

"Worried?" Mallory's voice emerged as a croak; her throat was as dry as sandpaper and it complained in a rasp as the words were spoken.

In truth, the situation was reversed. Naomi was not worried, in fact, she had planted the first seed of disquiet in Mallory by calling her to this office with no explanation. She had watered and fed that worry with the test result form on her desk. Now it was time to harvest the bounty. She needed to find out what Mallory had overheard the night before and glean as much as she could of her family's relationship with the Lees.

"Recently, you have been very forgetful," she swept a hand aside to indicate the abandoned bag of school clothes from the night before, "I know you came back for them, but it's very strange that you left them a second time,"

"Right," Mallory stubbornly stuck to monosyllabic responses. She realised what Naomi was doing – placing her outside the office door at the time of her meeting with Edith Morris. How could she have been clumsy enough to leave them a second time?

Keeping her mind clear was becoming a bit of a struggle. Those black and white letters to her left seemed to be growing to the size of the desk itself.

"You haven't been blacking out, have you?"

Mallory was startled by the bluntness of the seemingly unrelated question, "I don't understand,"

"Is that why you keep forgetting so many things? Episodes like this are usually symptoms resulting from-" a quick glance at that damned form, "other factors. Do you remember last night?"

The buzzing in her mind escalated, a signal of her rising fear, but the pressure allowed Mallory to think more clearly.

"Last night?" she repeated, a weak attempt to buy

herself more thinking time. Naomi was offering a choice. Denying memory of the night before would most likely lead Naomi to the belief that she was blacking out and the reason for that was surely on that test form. Mallory needed more information to know when that form was dated.

The other option was to admit that she remembered (of course she remembered!) but where would that lead her? A simple telling off for eavesdropping? Compared to the alternative, this decision was a no-brainer.

"Of course I remember last night,"

"So, you remember that I was in a meeting? And you remember that you deliberately listened at my door?"

Mallory instinctively blanched at the accusation, was too slow to convincingly sell her lie, "Of course I didn't,"

"You're a bad liar Miss Dunkeany,"

"I-"

"And it's not the only thing you've been lying about, is it?" Naomi reached across for the dreaded form. She managed to contain her feelings of satisfaction at Mallory's expression.

Chewing at the end of her braid in distress, Mallory stared bewildered at the form. She had lost this game they had been playing across the desk. Epically lost. She felt a charge building up in her palms. She was not used to losing. Give her a physical battle and Naomi wouldn't stand a chance.

"This is the result of a drugs test all the girls undertook recently, after those accusations were made at our last game," Naomi explained, "Yours is the only one to have returned positive for power enhancing drugs,"

It was impossible.

Mallory remembered taking the test. She clearly remembered dropping off her sample at the nurse's station. She definitely clearly remembered swapping her stickered name with Monica's. She had felt awful, but at the time she couldn't afford to let her secret out.

She felt less guilt now, knowing that had Cat been telling

the truth, Monica would have received a negative test result anyway.

Hopefully.

But that did not detract from the fact that there was a very realistic positive result sitting between her and Naomi. Mallory knew it wasn't true, but would anyone else know that? Who would believe her?

Naomi's threat hung like an ugly, thunderous cloud between them.

"Do you have anything to say for yourself?" she demanded.

Mallory could only shake her head. She was intent on preventing the situation from spiralling beyond her control. It was paramount that this lie did not get out – it would lead to too many other questions. She may be negative now, but that wasn't the case six months ago. How far back would they look?

"You realise the severity of the situation,"

"Yes,"

"Good," the form was set aside, designated to a drawer in Naomi's desk. She smiled, feigning reassurance, "We can move beyond this, I just need your help,"

"Okay,"

"What did you overhear last night?"

"All I heard was you talking to Ms Morris about her brother-in-law,"

"And?"

"That's it,"

"Have you told anyone?"

Mallory shook her head.

"Are you sure?" Naomi's hand drifted towards the closed drawer. Mallory's mind flitted back to her siblings the night before. How the buzzing in her veins had got the better of her, and she had spilled the entire encounter between Naomi and Ms Morris. She remembered Poppy recounting her chance interaction with Joseph Morris, and she also clearly remembered the promise she had made to

Poppy that she would not tell anyone about it.

But that was before everything had been put at risk. So, Mallory told her everything.

That evening, whilst sat at the kitchen table, Mallory absentmindedly powered the radio on and off. She stopped when Agatha shouted to her, confused by the sudden appearance and disappearance of voices. She fiddled with her pen, trying to focus on her work but her thoughts once again drifted back to her meeting with Naomi.

She felt guilt and shame. There was also the fear that she would still be reported despite what Naomi had promised. Naomi was a teacher, wasn't it her job to report drug use?

Promises.

Why was she so bad at keeping them?

She was roughly pulled from her thoughts when the door slammed, and a hectic Poppy whirled into the kitchen.

"How could you tell?" she demanded tearfully.

"Tell?" Mallory deliberately acted confused. Frustration was already bubbling in her chest at Poppy's dramatic entrance.

"You told them, didn't you? About Travis and I and what happened at Westgate? I asked you not to tell!"

"Do you hear yourself?" Mallory exclaimed, her temper flaring, "He could have hurt you or worse! I didn't have a choice," she continued defensively.

I didn't. I didn't have a choice.

Poppy ran trembling fingers over her head, pulling loose tendrils of hair from her bun, "I don't trust that family Mal," she explained, "I realise it's ridiculous to risk so much, but I can just sense it,"

Mallory glared, "It is ridiculous," she snapped.

"Have you ever actually spoken to Edith?" Poppy asked. A brief smug smirk flittered across her face as Mallory shook her head, but it quickly became serious again, "I had a meeting with her today. I was so scared. There is something about that woman, I was frozen when I spoke to her,"

Mallory remained unresponsive. Her icy, disbelieving glare caused a flurry of anger to boil over in Poppy, "Oh of course you wouldn't care!" she burst out, "Anything beyond your own little world isn't worth the effort!"

"The only reason I told anyone was to keep you safe!" Mallory barked. The lights above them flickered erratically, "I didn't have a choice!" she repeated.

"A choice?" Poppy sneered, "Of course you did!"

Cringing, Mallory was unable to meet Poppy's gaze. She couldn't know, surely? But it had been impossible for Naomi to know too. Her world was rapidly unspooling from her electrified fingertips.

Poppy pointed accusingly, "There was another reason, wasn't there? There was something in it for you! What was it? An A grade? Captain of the netball team?"

"I had no choice!" Mallory shrieked. A muffled pop. The entire house lit up blindingly like a solar flare before plunging into darkness.

"Mal," Poppy's voice whispered through the gloom, "Did you just blow the electrics?"

Mallory held her shaking hands to her head, they still tingled slightly. She had managed to keep this secret for so long, but now? She was losing control.

ESSENCE

Part 4
Thunder
15th November 2019

ESSENCE

CHAPTER 1
9:15 – The Dunkeany Residence

Poppy prepared to leave the house, a letter tucked firmly into her pocket. On learning how she discovered her powers, both Claire and Patrick had been uncomfortable with Edith Morris' involvement. They had elected to co-write a letter, thanking Edith for her help, but that it would be better for her daughter to come to terms with her newfound ability through psychotherapy sessions before returning to her regular visits. They neglected to mention their real intention: Poppy would never return if they could help it. Even they believed some of the rumours.

Poppy had already opened the envelope, read the letter and resealed it about three minutes after her parents had left the house that morning. She felt relief knowing that she would no longer have to visit Edith but feared her return to the dingy treatment room with Dr. Thackery.

"I'm going!" she shouted to her siblings. Mallory was tucked away in her room, diligently studying like she did every Saturday morning. After helping her replace the fuses following the 'flare incident', Mallory had barely spoken to her. The two sisters had barely spoken recently, their longest conversation having been in the car after Poppy's argument with Aaron.

"If I don't come back, it's probably because Edith has killed me," she jokingly called.

Aaron was sprawled in front of the television, waffle crumbs scattered across his t-shirt. She had exchanged so few words with him since their fight in the road, and he obstinately ignored her now. Poppy wrapped a scarf around her neck, sarcastically announcing, "Great to know I can rely on you guys,"

"I'm sure you'll be fine," he grunted.

Poppy's eyes narrowed, a tendril of anger sparking in her chest. She had been overwhelmingly upset at first as Aaron deliberately refused to talk to her, but it rapidly evolved into fury. His stubbornness had caused a rift in the household, leaving all of them unsettled over the last few weeks. Agatha was more disturbed and upset than usual, complaining of pooka sightings and that she could sense the Cóiste Bodha coming.

Aaron still spent most of his evenings out with his friends. Poppy struggled to hide her envy over how much time he was able to spend with Travis, resenting the discovery of the power.

The sooner she delivered this letter, the sooner things could go back to normal.

"You're seeing Mikey and Benj this afternoon, right?" she asked.

The non-committal grunt was her final straw. She stomped over to her brother and sharply slapped the back of his head, "This has gone on long enough!" she spoke coldly, fury rolling off her in waves, "Speak to me! What are you scared of?"

"I'm not scared of anything!" Aaron argued defensively. He pulled his knees up to his chest and stubbornly refused to take his eyes from the television screen.

"So why won't you look at me?"

"Did you read that article I sent you?" he asked,

changing the subject.

The question only made Poppy's anger rage more intensely, "You mean the one with all the death figures?" she spat. Aaron had seen fit to send her several articles. One listed the deaths caused by Organic Kinaesthetics during the war, another raving about how important it was to keep track of this power using the Organic Kinaesthetic Registry. The words had made her stomach turn.

"Is that all you see when you look at me?" she continued, unable to keep her voice from shaking with hurt, "Death tolls?"

A whimper interrupted their argument, Agatha's hands flurried over her face and chest in worry, "Death tolls?" she asked, "The tolls of death? The Cóiste Bodha is coming,"

Throwing an accusing glance at his sister, Aaron leapt from the sofa to comfort their grandmother. Poppy, feeling mortified for upsetting Agatha, quickly left the house, slamming the front door behind her.

The morning was unusually warm and humid. Large clouds hung heavy overhead, threatening a rare autumnal storm. With the letter weighing heavily in her pocket, Poppy set out towards the Morris' home, anxiety fizzing in her nerves. However, instead of following the route into town, she detoured.

Towards Travis' house.

She wanted to let Travis know as soon as possible that she would no longer be seeing Edith so they could go back to being friends.

When the front door to Travis' home opened, both Travis and his mother were hurriedly pulling coats and shoes on. Behind them, the interior of the house looked like it had been subjected to a tornado. Shattered pieces of crockery were scattered across the floor, dirt was trodden into the carpet, and the curtains that had concealed the front room for so long had been torn down.

Anna lunged forward to close the door on her, but Poppy leapt forward quicker, throwing herself into the gap,

"Please, I just need to say one thing!"

"We don't have time! We need to-"

Travis put a soothing hand on his mother's shoulder, "I'll talk to her, just give me two minutes. Please," He slipped through the gap in the door, leading Poppy by the elbow to the end of the garden.

"I'm not seeing her anymore!" she announced, tripping slightly as Travis dragged her. She waved the letter in his face, "I'm dropping this off, apologising and that's it. I'm done,"

"Look Poppy, I'm really sorry, this isn't a good time,"

She peered over his shoulder, at the dark, empty windows of his house. She realised the inside of the window were scorched black.

"What's happened, did you have a fire?" she gasped, "Was it...?"

"I will explain, I just can't right now," As he fumbled with the gate latch, she noticed bandages slipping from beneath his gloves.

"Will you come with me?" she begged.

He stopped, staring at her in disbelief, "Poppy, I can't drop everything for you," he told her angrily, "Look at my house! Don't you see I have other things to deal with right now?"

He turned away, preparing to join his mother again, when Poppy gripped him furiously. The obvious traumatic events that had occurred here had settled a limp of dread in the pit of her stomach. If she could get Travis to come with her, she was sure she could alleviate the weight of it.

"Seriously, I am scared. Scared that she is going to do to me what she did last time-"

"No!"

In that brief moment that Poppy held onto his arm, her hand erupted into burning colours of red and orange. It looked as if her skin was burning away, peeling to reveal the ugly, bloodied colours of her muscles on display.

Her grip only tightened and she felt the surging current

under Travis' skin. She could sense all the chromatophores streaming into her hand, and in that moment, she knew without a shadow of a doubt that she could divert them. Reverse them back into Travis' own hand, cause his skin to peel.

She whipped her hand back instinctively.

Unaware of what Poppy had felt, Travis believed her flinch was a result of the unintentional use of his power. He hadn't meant to change Poppy's hands into a reflection of his own, but after everything that had happened that day, he was unable to summon the energy to feel bad about it, "Look, I'm sure you'll be fine. She's an old woman and you have this brand new, super powerful ability. I'm sure if it came down to it, you could take her,"

"You've been spending too much time with Aaron," she responded bitterly.

"And if things go wrong, you can phone me," he continued, ignoring her, "And we can catch up and talk about this, okay?"

"Okay," she said softly, but he had already gone.

10:00 - The Morris Residence

Poppy's hand hovered above the door knocker. Her hands were shaking. What could she expect behind this door? How would Edith react? She pushed the possible futures from her mind, slammed the knocker down and held her breath.

Several minutes later the door had still not opened. Poppy considered just pushing the envelope through the letterbox and running. It was obvious no one was home, and she could wait here all day with no answer so she would be better off just pushing the envelope through....

Just as she lifted the flap of the letterbox, the door swung open, and Poppy almost fell into the hallway. Edith stood there, breathing raggedly. Wisps of hair had escaped her bun and they framed her face in a hectic tangle. A wailing voice flowed around her, blustering into Poppy and pushing her back a step.

"Poppy?" she said incredulously, "What are you doing here?"

"I, uh, have a letter," she stuttered, flustered by Edith's eccentric appearance, "From my parents. It's to let you know I'll no longer be coming to visit you," she pushed the envelope into Edith's hands. The wailing undulated, like a wave. She tried to ignore it, pushing images of Margaret's previous episode from her mind.

Edith took the letter gingerly. There were tender, red marks on her hands and blisters around her wrists.

"Your hands!" Poppy exclaimed without thinking.

Edith threw the letter aside, waving away the comment, "Your visits are no longer necessary, thank you for the courtesy call,"

The door slammed in her face.

She blinked, bewildered. She could not believe it had been that easy. She guiltily thanked Margaret for choosing that morning to have an episode. It obviously meant that Edith was too distracted to think about anything else.

Poppy hopped down the steps, a great weight lifted. Travis had been right. She kept her message to him curt: 'All fine just like you said, don't worry about meeting later'. The hurt from his words was still quite raw. She planned to go for a walk, perhaps in Westgate, to avoid the awkward tension of home.

As she sauntered through the gates of the Morris grounds, she began a second message on impulse. 'Edith's hands looked b-' but she was startled from finishing by a desperate "Psst!"

She glanced at the bushes beside the gate, looking for the source, absent-mindedly hitting send on her message without finishing. Arabella suddenly leapt from behind a tree, grabbing Poppy by the elbow and dragging her into her hiding spot. She was sweating and breathless, worry creasing her brow. Her pale eyes seemed glazed and desperate. Poppy tried not to recoil from her. Fear was practically oozing from Arabella's pores.

"Please," she hissed, pulling Poppy close, "You have to help my mother!"

CHAPTER 2
10:00 - Corbeck Town

Travis frowned at Poppy's cryptic message. Edith's hands looked what? He sent a single question mark in response before grumpily shoving his phone back into his pocket. He wanted to explain to her what had been happening to him over the past few weeks. He wanted to talk about Joseph's increased number of panic attacks and the intensity of his PTSD. How he lived with a potential criminal, and in a constant fear that his house would be burned down. About all the flawed plans he, Mikey and Benj had brainstormed so that he could see her again.

He wanted to apologise about not telling her about it all before, about the promise to his mother.

Then she had come to him, demanding comfort from him when he was at his breaking point. He just needed more time.

Stopping on a street corner, he collapsed on a bench. Burying his head in his hands, he wondered how the past week's events had led to this. Both he and his mother believed that Joseph had suffered an intense PTSD attack that morning, one that had resulted in a volatile eruption of his abilities that had wrecked the house and left scorch marks on the walls. He was now missing, and their top priority was to find him before he could hurt anyone else.

He could not help Poppy, not until he had found and helped his uncle first.

But there was no sign of Joseph! No ominous billows of smoke filling the sky, no fire engine sirens. It was impossible to find a man who had years of practice at hiding.

It was as Travis was running his hands through his hair in frustration that he saw it, the small, melted mark on the pavement. He crouched beside it, examining the mark. It was oblong, but curved, dipping in slightly in the middle. Travis pressed his finger against it, pushing his chromatophores through the material. It felt sticky, tugging at his skin. It glowed a bright yellow, contrasting cleanly against the grey of the pavement.

It was a footprint. A footprint created by the melted sole of a shoe.

Travis realised how precarious Joseph must be. He was heated enough that he was literally melting the rubber off the sole of his shoes. The tell-tale marks were distinct, leading away from the corner down a single lane.

The lane that led to the Morris household.

10:15 - The Morris Residence

Margaret writhed and wailed within her bedsheets. The noise was deafening. Poppy felt it wiggle into her ear, tearing strips away from her eardrums. The screaming reached a crescendo, and she felt incapacitated, sensing her knees crumple into the soft rug.

Arabella lay sprawled next to her mother, gripping onto her hand. Margaret was sweating profusely, her dark hair stuck damply in strands to her forehead. Her body convulsed with the sheer effort of screaming, her mouth gaping.

"You have to help my mother!" Arabella's words from the garden whirled around Poppy's mind, becoming entangled with the few discernible phrases Margaret was screaming.

"My mother!"
"You have to help-"
"My mother, she did-"
"Help!"
"Stop her!"

She crawled towards the bed, disorientated. Margaret's cries whisked around her, repeating and reversing and retreating until Poppy couldn't pull any tangible meaning from it. She was struggling to recall why she was even there. Why had she subjected herself to this torture?

She clawed at the mattress, hauling herself up against the noise. Arabella's pale and sickly face stared back at her, a sheen of sweat coating it. She was struggling against the noise too, helpless in the face of her mother's illness.

Arabella's expression of vulnerability pulled Poppy back to the task at hand. Shaking with the effort, she gently placed a hand on Margaret's forehead. She blindly felt for the current, but it was lost amongst the agony and pain. It fizzed and popped, jerking erratically and Poppy flailed in a vain attempt to catch it.

She couldn't do this. She didn't have enough practice. What if she hurt Margaret more by accident? Glancing up in panic, Poppy saw Arabella shouting something at her. But her voice was lost amongst the myriad of words tangled within Margaret's screams.

"I saw you!"
"My mother!"
"Help!"
"Save him!"
"Help him!"

Poppy clenched her jaw, pushing away the intruding words. She could try to make sense of them later. When it was quiet. She had to focus and calm Margaret.

In her subconscious, she again groped for the current. She managed to catch the trailing end, clutching it with her mind. Holding onto it, she could suddenly envision the flow of life within. It was panicked. Terrified.

Poppy drew a deep breath, separating herself from the room. The noise continued to batter her, bombarding her ears and making her teeth ache. But she was able to hold onto the current and push in a sense of calmness. She immediately sensed a change within the current, a softening. They no longer jolted like streaks of lightening, but wavered and shimmered.

Poppy built on the sense of calm, emphasizing it until Margaret's wails settled into strangled sobs. She felt relief wash over her as the room grew quiet. The air felt lighter now that the sound had been pulled from it. Her relief was quickly replaced with exhaustion however, as the use of her power quickly took its toll.

The two girls sat quietly together, basking in the newfound silence. It occurred to Poppy then, the absence of Edith. Why wasn't she here, trying to soothe her daughter? It was as she opened her mouth to ask that Margaret rose suddenly from her sheets, spooked. Her eyes, red and tear-stained, rolled in her head as she struggled to focus. She clutched her daughter's hands and exclaimed, "She did it! My mother, I saw her kill my father!"

CHAPTER 3
17th August 1979 - The Morris Residence

The air was warm and thick, weighed heavy by the suspense of a brewing storm. Despite the setting of the sun over the horizon, the temperature remained stifling hot. Margaret Morris, at four years old, played with her dolls in the gently swaying grass of the garden. Here she could avoid the nurse, hoarding the precious minutes before she was forced to bed. Her blonde hair, already beginning to darken, was swept back from her damp forehead, and the only noise to break the smothering, still air was the chirping of crickets.

Margaret swept her dolls across the grass, lost in her imagination, when another noise broke the evening silence. Raised voices could be heard, muted slightly by the humidity. The dolls stilled mid-dance. They dropped to the ground. Margaret rose to her feet and wobbled unsteadily towards the voices. The voices of her mother and father arguing.

The veranda doors to the study were open and the curtains swept aside in a vain attempt to encourage a breeze. Margaret settled on muddy knees beside the door, drenched in the shadows of the evening. A single table lamp illuminated the room. Some light escaped through the doors, creating a perfect rectangle on the floor outside.

Margaret eyed the three figures. Two were her parents, one a stranger. He was dressed mundanely, in a shirt and tie and blazer. She failed to recognise his face and her gaze slid over his ordinary features.

"I am proposing an unprecedented offer to you Mr Morris," the stranger was saying, exasperatedly pushing his glasses back up his nose, "One you will truly regret turning down,"

"I do not want to sell!" Nathaniel's voice was thunderous, causing Margaret to flinch in her hiding place, "I do not want this company to keep producing! It needs shutting down, we've caused too much damage,"

Margaret sensed a dissonance. Usually, when close to her father, she could hear some of his thoughts that he would project. But now, there was a worrying, muffled silence, as if something was supressing Nathaniel's outreach.

Edith clutched at her husband's shoulders, large rings glistening on her fingers. She wore a short, crêpe dress of Yves Saint Laurent's Libération collection. It was one of Margaret's favourites, she like the way the material felt between her fingertips.

"Can't you see how this money will look after us?" Edith demanded, "How it will make us financially stable?"

"It's none of your business Edith," Nathaniel replied grumpily. He stubbornly pushed the contract back across the desk to the stranger.

"I will not sign it," he reiterated, "I am closing down production of the Morris Mios," He rose from his seat, a sense of finality in the movement.

However, as he bid good evening to the stranger, he froze. Margaret watched her father awkwardly return to his chair, his limbs jerking like that of a puppet with a particularly vicious master. His face rapidly blushed vermillion as his hand reached out and shakily clasped a pen.

Edith stepped away from him impassively, allowing the

stranger to stand behind Nathaniel and gently place his bare fingertips on his temples. Nathaniel grasped the pen more firmly, and his movements flowed more smoothly as he signed the contract that would sell his company.

Margaret shrunk away from the door, confused by what was occurring. She thought her father didn't want to do that? Why was he doing it now the stranger was touching him? She sensed an immense pressure in the atmosphere, telling her that something was terribly wrong.

Finally, after a seemingly infinite amount of time, the pen finished scratching at the page and dropped from Nathaniel's fingers. But still the stranger did not release him.

"You know what happens now, don't you?" the stranger asked softly.

Edith nodded, "Yes," she said, not a single tremor in her voice.

"And you're content with it?"

"I've made my peace,"

Margaret stuffed her fist in her mouth and bit on her knuckles to prevent herself from screaming at what happened next. The stranger made a rolling motion with both hands, as if wrapping a rope around his hands, and suddenly snapped his fists away from Nathaniel's skull. There was an audible noise, one that little Margaret could not begin to comprehend, as her father's life current was ripped in half before her.

Nathaniel's eyes rolled momentarily before he slammed face first onto the desk.

Joseph Morris felt his brother die.

Nathaniel's psychic link, a constant buzzing at the base of Joseph's skull, blinked out. He hadn't noticed it over the past half an hour, it had been muffled and Joseph had assumed his brother was sleeping. But a deafening silence suddenly filled the void. He leapt from his books, and hurtled along the corridor, desperately searching rooms for his brother. He did not know at first, that he was dead.

He sped into the hallway, almost colliding with Edith in the hallway.

"Nathaniel!" he gasped at them, "Where is he?"

Edith's eyes widened in panic, and she glanced fearfully at her guest, "Why?" she managed.

"I need to find him, I think something terrible has happened!" Joseph rushed away from them, checking the front parlour before finally heading towards the study. He heard the front door slam, and the rushing footsteps of Edith follow him.

Margaret heard the running footsteps before they reached the room. Her trembling fingers touched her father's face one last time, before she ran. She hurtled away and out the open veranda doors, her legs careening wildly as she ran to her dolls. She clutched the dolls to her chest, her tears dampening their skirts.

Joseph held his brother's face in his palms, unable to comprehend the feeling of loss. He did not look up as Edith entered the room, nor acknowledge her gasp of horror. He felt the familiar heat in his hands, and finally let go. He did not want to mark his brother.

"Jay," Edith covered her face with shaking hands, "What did you do?"

Joseph turned to her, bewildered, "What do you mean?"

She simply gestured at the scene before her.

"Edith no, this wasn't me," Joseph pleaded, "How can it have been me? I was just looking for him,"

"How did you know this had happened?" she questioned, adding tremulous lilt to her words, "You knew,"

"He has a psychic link Edith, that's his ability! I felt it cut off,"

"I didn't feel anything," she said softly, accusingly.

"I didn't do this!" Joseph shouted. His anger fuelled the heat in his palms, and it added to the already uncomfortable warmth of the room.

"You're scaring me!" Edith cried out unexpectedly.

Joseph stumbled away from her, confused by her reaction.

"Somebody help!" she cried out again before turning to Joseph, "I love you Jay, but you have to understand that this doesn't look good,"

"I didn't do this, you have to believe me!"

"What do you expect me to do?" she viciously snapped, "I catch you next to my dead husband!"

"The doors are open! It could have been anyone!" Desperation began to murkily merge with his anger, confusing and panicking him. Would they believe Edith? Would they believe that he could have done this?

Footsteps once again echoed in the hallway, becoming louder as they reached the study. Joseph felt himself lose his grip on his thoughts. They rushed away from him, refusing to stay still long enough for him to make sense of them. Through all his pain and suffering from the loss of his brother to the horrors of the war, all he could focus on was one word. Run!

Joseph ran. He flew through the windows, too blinkered to see the sly smile soften Edith's lips. Once again, unknown to Joseph, he was suffering through his first post-traumatic stress episode. He managed to get as far as Westgate trainyard before collapsing. In his terror, he lay down as flames erupted uncontrollably around him.

CHAPTER 4
25th November 2019 - 10:40

The Morris Residence

In the eerie silence that followed Margaret's announcement, the two girls cowered. If what Margaret was saying was true, Poppy thought hysterically, and Edith had been involved in Nathaniel's death, that meant she had been spending time with a murderer. That she was currently in the same house as a killer.

"What do we do?" Arabella whispered fearfully. Her eyes darted from her mother, who had collapsed into a fitful but quiet sleep, to the door. They both remained tense, as if Edith would suddenly appear.

Poppy returned the wide-eyed stare, too terrified to speak. She could only shrug and shake her head.

The silence was shattered by a series of thumps and shouts from above their heads, causing the girls to flinch and duck beneath the bed. The deafening noise continued as they huddled in the dusty crawl space under the bed. It emanated from the attic and caused cracked ceiling plaster to rain down.

"What is that?" Poppy hissed through clenched teeth. She fumbled for her phone in her back pocket, causing dust to spiral in the confined space. It crawled up Arabella's nose and made her sneeze.

"I don't know," Arabella said thickly, wiping the dust from her nose, "There's been noises like that all morning, I think it's what disturbed my Mama so much,"

A particularly fierce yell caused both girls to flinch again. To Poppy, it sounded like someone was in pain.

"We have to see who it is, someone might be hurt," she decided, pulling herself out onto the bedroom floor.

"No, you can't!" Arabella gripped her ankle, "There's a man up there, he'll hurt you!"

Poppy jerked viciously, pulling her leg free, "By the sounds of it, he's hurting someone else!" she argued.

Arabella curled into a ball, shaking her head and muttering. Poppy left her there, conscious that she may be running out of time. As she stood up, the faint smell of smoke caressed her senses. She unlocked her phone, barely noticing Travis' response, and tapped 999. Holding the phone steadily to her ear as it began to ring, she moved carefully into the hallway, following the sound of the noise.

"Hello? Which emergency service do you require?"

The thick smell of smoke assaulted her senses. Poppy could see it billowing out from beneath the attic door at the end of the hallway. She floundered momentarily in the wake of the calm voice, uncertain whether to say fire service or ambulance.

"I think there's a fire," she said finally.

"Okay, I'm passing you on to the fire service now,"

The cries were much louder now, consisting of layers of pain, fear and anger. Poppy found herself frozen at the base of the staircase, unable to move forward. The smoke was noxious, it felt like someone was pressing stinging needles into her eyes.

"Hello, this is the Fire Service, what is the postcode?" a voice spoke calmly in her ear. It felt disorientating, contrasting so greatly against the screaming from above.

"I'm at the Morris Household, by Westgate Forest," she stuttered, "I think there's a fire in the attic? There's a lot of smoke,"

The voice continued in her ear, speaking soothingly. However, she stopped listening when the attic door swung open. Great clouds of smoke flowed from the confined space, and two figures emerged, bent double and coughing. Poppy quickly recognised Edith's silhouette, but she couldn't see the second clearly through the dense smog.

"We need to calm him," the figure gasped, wafting the smoke away from their face, "I can't do anything if he keeps combusting!" The voice was eerily familiar, evoking the sense of isolation she felt so often as a child. Where had she heard that voice before?

Edith continued coughing into a handkerchief, "I just need some air!" she choked, "Then I'll pause him long enough for us to deal with this," she waved her hand, indicating the flaming room behind them, "Then we'll try again,"

She paused when she saw Poppy, standing slack-jawed with the phone still pressed to her ear.

"Who's that?" the voice demanded from inside the room.

In response, Edith gaped for a moment before collecting herself, "A loose end," she said coldly.

Poppy suddenly felt the familiar squeezing sensation on her chest and shoulders. Edith was pausing her! She lurched backwards in an attempt to break the connection. Whirling away, she flung her phone at Edith with outstretched fingers. It flew upwards, arcing through the smoky air as a tinny voice asked repeatedly for the nature of the fire.

Edith ducked. The phone flew past her, cracking against the door frame. But it was enough of a distraction. The link between Edith and Poppy snapped. Poppy willed her legs into motion. She turned her back to the door and ran for the stairs. She felt something tug at her subconscious, as if fingertips were tugging lightly at her, trying to pull her back. She easily shrugged the sensation away as she pounded down the stairs towards the front door.

Travis had followed the melted rubber footprints to the gates of his Grandmother's house. He stood shaking, peering between the twisted metal as smoke poured from beneath the eaves of the house. He knew Joseph was in there. It was no coincidence that this house was on fire so shortly after Joseph went missing.

Poppy's cryptic message suddenly made sense. The 'b' probably meant 'burned'. Why didn't she finish the message?

He tugged at the gates and was surprised when they swung easily inwards. He pulled up his mother's number, but before he could press the ring icon the front door of the house flew open with a resounding crack that echoed throughout the garden.

"Poppy?!" Travis yelled incredulously as she ran down the gravel pathway towards him. She seemed just as startled to find him there as he her.

"Travis?" her chest heaved as she slowed to a stop. She had lost both her scarf and coat and was now shivering in her thin jumper. She was also covered in dust.

"What the hell happened to you?" he demanded.

Her eyes were wide and frightened, and she was at a loss at how to begin explaining. Now she was closer, he could smell the distinct odour of smoke.

"We need to get away," she managed, "I need to get away from her,"

"I thought you said it had gone fine?" he questioned, "You text me, remember?"

She shook her head, trembling as she tried to supress tears, "It did, and then Arabella pulled me back in because her Mum was having an episode so I calmed her down like I did before and then-" She dissolved into tears as she remembered Margaret's revelation, "Then she said that

ESSENCE

Edith had killed your Grandad and then the attic was on fire and she tried to pause me again and..." her voice trailed off into sobs as she covered her face with her hands.

Travis tugged her into a tight hug, his brain whirling. The smoggy smell of smoke coated the back of his throat. There was supposed to be a meeting this morning, at the trainyard. Aaron would be there. Travis could easily deliver his sister to him and be back here in time to help Joseph.

He pushed Poppy away from him, tenderly wiping her eyes, "Let's get you to Aaron," he said firmly, "We were supposed to be meeting up this morning, so I know where he is," He rang his mother, but the call went straight to voicemail. He left a garbled message and sent a text for good measure.

"Okay," Poppy nodded, sniffling. He quickly wrapped her in his own jacket, then took her by the hand and led her towards Westgate. She meekly followed, exhausted by the events of the past hour. Travis shifted focus to helping her, desperately hoping that by the time he got back, he would find his mother with everything under control.

All he had to do right now was find Aaron.

CHAPTER 5
11:30 - The Dunkeany Residence

Aaron was late. He was supposed to be on his way to Westgate for another training session, but he had unintentionally drifted back to sleep in front of the television. Now time was running rapidly short, and he was hurriedly setting out Agatha's medication for the afternoon like he had promised.

"Right Nan," he said as he set the timer, "Your tablets are all there for you. Your timer is set, Mallory will be down in a bit to check you've had them, okay?"

She stared at him blankly, "Okay dear,"

He picked up the remote, flicking through the channels, "Is there anything you want to watch? The end of Saturday Kitchen?" he suggested.

"Oh!" Agatha excitedly picked up her TV schedule, "There's a Christmas film on Channel 5," she tapped her the paper, showing where she had circled the film.

"Nan, it's November!"

"Is it?"

Aaron felt the pit of his stomach drop as he realised; jokes like that didn't land anymore.

"Yeah," he said softly, "But if you want to watch Christmas films, you can,"

Finally, with the television set to Channel 5 and an extra jumper on, he was ready to leave. As he walked into the hall, the doorbell rang. He threw his head back and groaned in annoyance.

"Mal!"

"Answer it yourself!" was the muffled response.

Aaron rolled his eyes and opened the door to find a well-dressed man on the doorstep.

"Good morning," the man smiled. Aaron recognised him but was unable to place him until he introduced himself, "I'm Dr Thackery. I'm here to see Poppy,"

Aaron gawped briefly. He had not seen this man for several years. He looked older now, his hair had begun greying, but there were the same piercing eyes behind the glasses. He wrinkled his nose at the smell of smoke emanating from Thackery's clothes, maybe he had taken up smoking in the intervening years?

"On a Sunday?"

Thackery nodded stiffly, and Aaron was amused to see his left eye quiver with a tick of annoyance.

"Yeah, she's not in," Aaron said, beginning to push past him, "Look, I need to be somewhere, so if you'll excuse me,"

Thackery placed a firm hand on his shoulder, stopping him in his tracks, "Are you parents not home?"

"No," Aaron responded, harshly shrugging him off. The acrid smell of smoke assaulted his nostrils.

"It's really important that I find your sister," Dr Thackery continued, forcing his way forwards into the house. Aaron scowled; an alarm began ringing violently in the back of his mind.

"Why? What's wrong with her?"

He nonchalantly leaned against the wall, pressing his palm firmly against it behind his back. He outwardly exhibited a calm, almost disinterested demeanour, but in reality, he was urgently sending vibrations through the walls of the house, targeted at Mallory's room. His mixed feelings regarding his twin were quickly smothered by the fear that she could be hurt or in danger. Even if Mal didn't get the message, he hoped he could annoy her enough for her to come storming down the stairs.

"Well, on discovery of her new powers, we need to get an evaluation session set up immediately," Thackery spoke smoothly, but slowly, as if he was deliberately dumbing down the sentence. It made Aaron's temper flare, and he produced a particularly violent vibration that caused the picture frames to rattle.

He heard several books hit the floor above him, and the lights flickered on for a second.

"Bet that was a bit of a shock huh? Spending all those years with her and not noticing," Aaron commented drily, an edge of derision in his tone.

"Quite," Thackery glanced at the frames and ceiling, his tone perturbed.

"Look, you'll have to come back another time, she's not here," Aaron's phone buzzed in his pocket as he spoke, and he habitually pulled it out and glanced at the message. It was a message from Travis to their group chat, demanding to know where Aaron was. He explained he had an upset Poppy with him, and he needed to get over himself and get his ass down there.

Thackery noticed the change in Aaron, the slight alteration in his body language depicting that the message he was reading was important.

"Is that her?" he demanded.

"What?" Aaron responded distractedly. He was focused on tapping out a response: Running late, Thackery's here and I can't leave until he does. Is she okay?

Thackery reached out to grab the phone, but Aaron jerked back, his reflexes automatically kicking in from the many times Mallory had snatched his phone to read his messages to girls. It still made him laugh that the messages she was really looking for wouldn't be found in any inboxes with girls.

"Give me the phone," Thackery held his palm out expectantly.

"No," Aaron tried to back away, but he felt something ugly tugging at him, holding him in place. He tried to call to Mallory, but he felt his vocal cords lock. His eyes widened in fear as Thackery stepped forward and held his jaw between firm fingertips. Through the contact of skin, Aaron felt himself lose all control. All the neurons carrying messages from his brain were re-directed, disturbed from their natural routes. Thackery was giving them to new destinations, and Aaron felt his arm move as it handed Thackery the phone.

He wanted to scream. What Thackery was doing was painfully violating. He realised, at last, that Thackery was an Organic Kinaesthetic. His brain fumbled through the contradicting pieces of information, but overriding it was the realisation that Poppy could be capable of something like this.

But that she wouldn't.

Thackery deftly scrolled through Aaron's messages, shifting his hold to the back of Aaron's neck with his other hand, his thumb still digging into his jaw.

"So, she's with Travis," he turned to Aaron, "Where is this train yard?"

Aaron felt his vocal cords loosen, but clenched his jaw, stubbornly not answering. How many times had a situation like this haunted him? How long had he been practicing for this? He wanted to look upwards, to see if Mallory was coming, but he was locked in position, holding eye contact with Thackery.

"Of course, you're not going to tell me that easily," Thackery clenched his fingers, digging his nails into Aaron's neck. Again, he felt the violating sensation of Thackery re-directing his neurons, and suddenly he could not catch his breath. His lungs felt like lead, heavy and immovable. He wanted to clutch at Thackery's arms, send some shockwaves through his system or pressurise his ear drums. But he was frozen.

Thackery wedged him against the living room doorway, asking again, "Where is the train yard?"

Black spots began encroaching on Aaron's vision. If he didn't get some air soon, he was going to pass out. He opened his mouth and Thackery allowed him enough breath to murmur "Westgate," before the TV remote smacked Thackery on the side of the head.

Then the bombardment began.

Random items from around the living room began a full-frontal attack on Thackery. Several books from the shelves, ornaments from the mantel piece, even a vase. The onslaught allowed enough time for Aaron to pull free from Thackery's grip, but he was still too weak from the lack of oxygen and crumpled to the floor.

Thackery lurched forward, attempting to locate the source of the barrage. Agatha sat serenely, her wrinkled face plastered with a smile, fingers swiping the air before her. She guided each living room missile directly at Thackery.

As he brought his arm up to protect himself, Thackery stumbled backwards into the waiting hands of Mallory. Her fingertips crackled with electricity, and she clapped her hands to his temples. He spasmed momentarily, before collapsing to the ground.

Aaron lay still on the floor, basking in his ability to control his own body again. He took in great gulps of air, enjoying the feeling of his lungs expanding and contracting. He twisted towards his grandmother, "Thanks Nan,"

Agatha smiled as she settled back beneath her blankets, "I can't lose you," she said, "Who else am I going to watch television with?"

Mallory reached down to help Aaron off the floor, but a spark jumped between their fingertips, "Oops, sorry, still some charge left," she apologised. She touched her fingertips to the ground and then pulled Aaron to his feet.

ESSENCE

She held him as he recovered. She knew he was scared because he did not push her away.

"What the hell happened?" she asked softly.

"I think I nearly died," he mumbled. The ragdoll Chikara player was unbelievably clear in his mind, and it was wearing his face. He had been training himself for so many years, and he had completely failed when it actually mattered.

"I wouldn't have let that happen," Mallory planted a kiss on his forehead, which embarrassed him enough to pull out of her embrace.

"Ugh," he muttered, rubbing his hair. He glanced down at the inert body of Dr Thackery, and the chaos of smashed ornaments that surrounded him. The use of her powers had exhausted Agatha, and she had already drifted off into a doze.

"We need to move him," Mallory decided, rolling up her shirt sleeves.

"I can do it," Aaron said tiredly.

"Aaron, you cannot lift a middle-aged man by yourself!" Mallory began to argue but she felt the words die in her throat as Aaron planted his feet and slowly lifted Thackery's body using vibrating air particles.

"How the hell did you learn to do that?" she demanded. She crouched down, staring at the gap between Thackery and the floor. The air seemed hazy, and a warmth emanated from it as the particles vibrated crazily.

"I've done heavier," Aaron guided him to the front door. Thackery's body wobbled continuously as the particles vibrated beneath him, dishevelling his combed hair, and knocking his limbs against the door frames. He dumped his body outside, behind their bins, where the worst of the autumnal leaf build up was.

"Heavier?" Mallory demanded.

Aaron shrugged, exhausted, "You'll see,"

CHAPTER 6
11:30 – Westgate Train Yard

The graffitied trains stood like sentries in the gloom. The dull daylight, already dimmed by the thunderous clouds, barely filtered into the clearing. Travis helped Poppy clamber over the tracks, comically bowing as he held her hand when she jumped the puddles.

Although still shaken from what she had learned, Poppy found herself feeling peaceful amongst the trees. This forest was a place where she would come whenever she felt upset or stressed. It had always been like that. There was something comforting about being shielded by trees.

They entered a gravel clearing to find Mikey and Benji batting rotten apples with a two by four. Mikey threw the apples at breakneck speeds, powered by air currents, and Benji barely had time to swing before the apples splattered against the makeshift bat.

"Have either of you seen Aaron yet?" Travis asked as another apple was spattered into oblivion.

Benji shook his head, "I haven't even heard from him for the past hour, he's ignoring my messages,"

"Useless," Travis muttered, aggressively sending a

message to Aaron. He noted, with some trepidation, that his mother hadn't responded to his calls and that his phone's battery was worryingly low.

Mikey began absent-mindedly juggling some of the apples form his collected pile, "It's not like he's ever on time," he added.

Travis quickly thumbed out a message to Aaron before turning to Poppy, "I need you to stay here,"

"Why? Where are you going?" she demanded.

"I need to go back,"

"Back?" Poppy responded incredulously, "You can't, it's too dangerous! The attic was on fire!"

Mikey dropped his juggling apples and hurried over at the word 'fire'.

"What was on fire?"

"The attic!" Poppy snapped, as if that explained it.

"That fire is my Great Uncle," Travis ran his hands frustratedly through his hair, "That's why I need to go back,"

"Hold up," Mikey interjected, "How is the fire your uncle?"

"Great Uncle," Benji corrected automatically.

"The man in the woods!" Poppy exclaimed, her eyes wide as the jigsaw pieces fell into place, "That was your Great Uncle Joseph, who was accused of murdering your Grandad but he didn't actually do it, Edith did!"

"Travis, man, you family is wild,"

Travis squeezed the bridge of his nose, "You said Margaret told you that?"

She nodded eagerly.

"She's ill, you can't take her word for it,"

"You can't go back there, you don't know how dangerous Edith could be! Or that stranger that she was with!"

"I am going Poppy, he needs my help!"

Benji and Mikey's head whipped back and forth between the quarrelling pair, as if they were watching a very intense tennis match.

"Perhaps you should listen to her," Benji suggested. It was possible to sense the rising tension between them even without his power.

"No, Benj, I need you and Mikey to keep her safe until Aaron gets here," Travis said firmly.

With that, he stormed away amongst the trains. He would follow the tracks, turning left at the fork that led to the dead end, and the Morris property. Poppy made to follow him, but Benji grabbed her by the wrist. An overwhelming wave of her emotions flooded into him, a difficult mix of grief, confusion, guilt and fear.

"Benji, you have to let me go!"

"We'll wait until Aaron gets here," Benji decided, "But in the meantime, you can tell us everything that's been happening,"

Mikey nodded vigorously, "I have many questions,"

The three of them sat on a log at the edge of the clearing. Mikey fluttered leaves into the air as Poppy began to explain everything that had happened. She began with an explanation of how she had suddenly developed powers, which both Mikey and Benji naturally already knew, thanks to Aaron. She told them about how Arabella had pulled her into the Morris' home to help her mother who had proceeded to tell them that Edith had actually killed Nathaniel, and not Joseph.

When she had finished, Mikey emitted a low whistle, "That's crazy," was all he managed. Poppy rested her head in her hands, exhausted from reliving the tale.

"So, Travis has gone back to get his Great Uncle," Benji summarised, more to himself than anyone, "But why is Mrs Morris going to such extremes to keep him?"

Poppy shrugged, "I suppose something to do with the murder, a confession maybe?" she speculated.

"Personally, I think we should go help him," Mikey proposed.

"Same," Poppy glared pointedly at Benji.

"I think we should wait,"

"That's two to one though!" Mikey argued playfully.

"No,"

They lapsed into a brief silence, before curiosity go the better of Poppy, "So when Aaron kept disappearing all those times, he was coming here?" She gestured to the dilapidated trains.

Mikey nodded, puffing his chest out in pride, "This is where we train twice a week. Me and Aaron, we can lift a whole carriage see, and that's before Benji's help,"

"Twice a week? Aaron's been sneaking out at least four nights a week," she frowned at the blatantly incorrect maths, "Where has he been going all those other nights?" she tailed off.

She missed as Mikey raised his eyebrows at Benji, as she became distracted by the train carriages, "You can lift a whole carriage?" she paused, "For Chikara?"

Mikey nodded, fiddling with his cap, "Guessing Aaron hasn't said much?"

"We haven't really spoken since he found out about me,"

"Aaron wants nothing more than to be part of Chikara," Benji begins to explain, "But he is afraid that one of us would get hurt. He's obsessed over it for years, analysing matches that have gone terribly wrong. He learned in the early years, before they were banned, that Organic Kinesthetics were the biggest cause of deaths. He does care for you still, he's just scare,"

"And stupid," Mikey added.

Poppy nodded absentmindedly. She was distracted by the fact that Travis had returned to that house without her. She needed to go help him.

"I think I just need to find somewhere to, y'know, go to the toilet," she lied.

Benji smiled gently, believing she just needed a moment to collect herself, "Sure, no problem" He and Mikey faced the other way, waiting patiently as the sound of Poppy's footsteps faded into the undergrowth.

Fifteen minutes later, Benji began to doubt himself.

Mikey voiced his concerns, "I don't think she's coming back,"

CHAPTER 7
12:00 - The Morris Residence

Poppy emerged from the edge of the forest breathing heavily. She had run all the way here, worried that either Benji or Mikey would catch on that she had not gone for a wee in the forest but, in actual fact, abandoned them to help Travis.

She darted around the perimeter of the garden wall, slid quietly through the front gate, before sprinting across the grass of the front lawn. She paused at a window, gasping for breath. She peered searchingly in. Her breath quickly fogged the glass, but she could still see clearly enough that the room was empty.

"Poppy?" She flinched at the sound of a familiar voice. She turned to find her old counsellor and surprise overwhelmed her fear of getting caught.

"Dr Thackery?" she stared, perplexed. She was unable to combine her two distinctly different worlds together. Here she stood, in Edith Morris' flowerbed, suspiciously peering through a window. Yet her childhood counsellor had inexplicably appeared before her.

Thackery smelt faintly of rotting leaves, dustbins, and bonfires. His hair was dishevelled, and his coat was stained.

She winced at the large welt on his temple.

"Poppy Dunkeany!" he seemed disturbingly happy to see her. He did not question the situation he found her in, with mud flecked up her socks and her hair loose and windswept. That was her first warning. He used to question her about everything.

"Why are you here?" she blurted, stepping briskly out of the mud and onto the path, feigning innocence.

"I could ask you the same question," he chuckled, adjusting his glasses so they no longer sat quite as askew, "I was very pleased to hear about the development of your ability," he continued.

Finding herself floundering a little in the strangeness of the exchange, Poppy felt her anxiety levels begin to rise. She had, admittedly, arrived at the Morris house uncertain of what to expect, but this was definitely not on the list of possible circumstances.

Thackery seemingly detected this and soothingly said, "We need to stay calm," But the words echoed in her mind, pulling her back to the base of the attic staircase only hours before.

"You were there," she faltered, instinctively stepping away.

"What do you mean?"

"This morning, the fire in the attic, you were there with Edith," she pressed her palms against her temples as she tried to make sense of the situation. She began muttering to herself, pulling all the little scraps of clues together in her mind.

"Why are you helping Edith? Why are you even here?" she muttered, more to herself than anyone.

Thackery sighed in exasperation, "We are stopping murderer from going free," he stated, "Of course, it's well known that he is responsible,"

She could only shake her head, "That's not true,"

Thackery's countenance suddenly changed, tensing at her words, "You know, Travis said the same thing," he commented through gritted teeth.

Poppy immediately demanded, "Where's Travis?"

"Come with me," he began to walk away, but she refused to follow him. She sensed his frustration at her disobedience.

"I don't trust you,"

The words had escaped her before she had time to consider them. But she realised that she had felt like this ever since she had first walked into his therapy room, and for all those years that had followed with her sitting in that sad little chair.

"We're not so different, you and I," he said softly, before his arm suddenly snapped out like a striking snake and grasped her elbow.

As he gripped her arm, there was that tugging again, the fingertips pulling at her subconscious. She pushed them irritably away and as she did so, Thackery was unable to hide his surprise.

Pieces once again fell into place for Poppy. Thackery was an Organic Kinaesthetic too, she realised. She felt disgust rise up like bile in her chest, "We have the same power?"

"Of course," he responded as if it was obvious, "You really think I would have wasted all that time on someone who didn't have an ability?"

Too distressed by the revelations, she allowed herself to be dragged into the house. Her entire childhood and adolescent had been spent as an outsider, actively encouraged by this man who was supposed to have been helping her.

In the hallway, Poppy stubbornly dug her heels into the floor, "Why?" she asked, hurt, "Why lie to me all that time? You were supposed to look out for me!" she cried angrily, jabbing a finger in his chest, "You were my therapist for God's sake!"

Thackery's face donned a mask of compassion as he spoke in an infuriatingly patronising manner, "I never claimed to be a therapist Poppy, only a man of guidance, to help you navigate a world that would never accept you. You are still going to be treated as an outsider with this ability. People are blinkered, they do not understand the potential, they fear it. They are going to fear you. Therefore, it was important you were trained to handle that,"

"Trained!" Poppy repeated hotly. Trained! Like an animal! "I am not some sort of pony that will perform tricks for you!" she continued furiously.

"I'm sure with a little encouragement you'll be happy to do as I ask," Thackery smiled as he guided her into the parlour.

Neither Thackery nor Poppy noticed Arabella crouched at the top of the staircase, listening intently to their exchange. She feared the stranger terribly. He was the one who had separated her from her sister. Whilst admiring Poppy's defiance, Arabella felt a boldness all her own beginning to blossom.

Both Travis and Joseph sat stiffly on the settee. It took Poppy a moment to realise that Edith had the pair frozen. Joseph appeared to be in a state of sleep, his head hanging heavily against his chest. Despite not being able to move, Travis' power continued relentlessly. The ornate satin cover of the settee pulsed an angry red hue, reflecting his fury at what was occurring. Flecks of black discoloured it as Travis caught sight of Poppy, his fear apparent in their erratic movement.

"Look who I found!" Thackery announced cheerfully, shedding his coat, and throwing it over the back of a chair. Edith stood, visibly trembling, as she maintained control. More wisps of hair had escaped her bun and her eyes were becoming bloodshot from the effort.

"There's too many people," she grunted.

"I thought you could handle this Edith," Thackery retorted sardonically.

Edith's eyes narrowed in a fury, but she shifted position

and summoned the last dregs of her energy, "Fireman, police! Anna is near the property too, we don't have much time,"

"Right Poppy, I want you to help Joseph sign his confession," Thackery dictated, "He's being a little stubborn at the moment,"

Joseph's hands were currently submerged in bowls of iced water to prevent him from spontaneously combusting again, "Why are you wasting your time with her?" Edith demanded.

"I have other priorities," Thackery said calmly. He turned to Poppy, "You understand what I'm asking of you?"

Despite her stomach lurching, she managed to shake her head. She remembered the fear in Aaron's eyes the night she had manipulated the tree, the promise she had made that she would never use her powers to control a person, and make them do something that they didn't want to.

"Yes," she answered, "But I won't do it,"

"This is an important step in your growth,"

"No,"

A disappointed sigh escaped from him. His hands twisted in the air as she concentrated and suddenly Travis began to convulse. Poppy lurched forwards to help him, but Thackery held her back.

"No no no," she desperately cried, "Please don't, don't!"

Thackery held Travis' lungs in stasis, preventing them from expanding and contracting, preventing him from breathing. He clutched at the carpet, colours radiated from his fingertips in a dizzying, kaleidoscopic tangles as he dug into the plush carpet. She watched his spasming chest in horror as he desperately tried to fill his lungs with air.

"Please stop!" she screamed, "You're hurting him!"

But Thackery refused to relieve the pressure.

Long fingers dug into Poppy's shoulders, holding her firmly in place.

"You must realise the true potential of your powers

Poppy," he hissed, rottenness on his breath, "Encourage him, help Joseph sign the confession,"

"I can't," Poppy whispered. Edith's eyes flickered erratically from Poppy, to Joseph, to Travis' writhing form on the floor. Poppy, unable to look away from Edith as her composure disintegrated, found herself reluctantly falling into her role as Thackery's patient, confiding in him despite his deceit.

"I'll be crossing a line," she murmured, "I promised I wouldn't,"

"No Poppy, what's not right is restricting yourself for the benefit of other people,"

She continued trying to pull away from Thackery, but his grip was too strong. She desperately searched the room for something when her eyes settled on Joseph. He finally appeared to have woken, and he held her gaze firmly. An understanding passed between them. He nodded once.

"Stop!" Joseph's voice clearly through the room. Despite his hands still being submerged in the buckets of ice water, a heat radiated from him.

"Stop this madness, I'll sign it," a sense of stoicism, of self-sacrifice had descended over him, "Willingly," he added.

"Oh Poppy," Thackery sighed, "You are such a disappointment," He pushed her aside, his focus entirely on Joseph.

Edith gasped suddenly, and the heavy blanket controlling the room suddenly lifted. Joseph was released, but he remained still. With an edge to his voice, Thackery asked "Who have you released?"

She collapsed into a chair, her face grey and drawn, "All of them," Thackery waved his hand dismissively at her. He was close to his goal now, the people around him were rapidly becoming irrelevant.

Edith blanched, seemingly seeing her grandson for the first time. Amongst violent coughing, Travis managed to draw a hoarse breath. Poppy dropped to her knees beside him, gently laying her hands on his shoulders. She focused on his lungs, helping them expand and contract for maximum airflow. Thackery's words assaulted her suddenly. With a sickening jolt, she realised how easily it could be for her to stop his breathing, to freeze the intercostal muscles or to shut down his lungs. Was she crossing a line even now, by helping Travis to breathe?

As soon as his breath settled, and Travis had stopped gasping for breath, Poppy pulled her hands away, fearful of their ability.

"You owe me this Joseph," Thackery murmured quietly, threateningly, "Sign it now,"

As the clock chimed the hour, Joseph brought the pen to the page with a shaking hand.

At the same time, Arabella attacked Edith from behind and the rear wall of the garden exploded.

12:55 - Outskirts of the Morris Estate

Volunteer firefighter, Robert Downing, was suddenly able to move again. He stretched his limbs, confused by his brief inanimation. He failed to recall what had come over him. Had he blacked out? How long had he been stuck?

He shook his head of the troublesome thoughts. He remembered why he was here. A possible fire. He continued forwards, hurrying worriedly now that he could see smoke in the sky. It coiled upwards, blending in with the thunderous clouds.

The call from the young girl had caused some consternation at the volunteer fire department, even more so when the call had unexpectedly cut off. They had sent Robert to investigate as a precaution, but now he could see there really was a problem.

Over his shoulder, he was relieved to see a police car barrel around the corner, and he waved it down. A skinny officer was in the driving seat, but a civilian woman sat beside him.

"Is there a fire?" she demanded.

Downing nodded, pointing to the smoke, "I'm ringing for backup now,"

"Get in," ordered the officer. As Downing slipped into the back, he said, "I'm glad you folks turned up, I've just had a funny turn,"

"A funny turn?" the woman whirled around in her seat and started intently at him, "How do you mean?"

Downing faltered slightly under her gaze, "Must have blacked out or something," he suggested weakly, "But then again, I remember just standing…"

The woman turned to the officer, "That'll be her,"

Downing called for backup from the rear of the police car. As they pulled up to the gates and clambered out the car, they could hear a faint rumbling, that gradually grew to a crescendo. He recognised it as the rhythmic shunting of a train barrelling too quickly along its tracks.

13:03 - The Morris Estate

Mallory blinked dazedly. Their plan had worked.
Sort of.

The train had got them to Morris' home in record time. They had not intended to come crashing through the wall, however. The four of them clambered disorientated from their sheltered hiding place and surveyed the mess before them.

The red brick dust began to settle across the debris. Mounds of mortar and bricks lay scattered about the destroyed train. The sound of screeching and rendering metal echoed in Mallory's ears, and she had to shake her head to rid herself of the ringing. They just hadn't been able to brake in time.

She vaguely remembered lights. Soft marsh lights, on the tracks, like glowing orbs, dancing lazily across her vision. They had unconsciously started to follow them…

Then the charred roof of the Morris house had come into view, the fire finally out. And Mallory had raised her fist to celebrate. And then the wall had appeared.

"Everyone okay?" she called, the last of the lights fading into forgotten obscurity. There were some mumbled confirmations in response, interjected with Mikey's hysterical laughter.

"That was awesome!" he crowed.

A hoarse cry resounded across the lawn, "What have you done to my garden?!" Edith screamed, "That's my wall!"

"We're here for my sister!" Aaron yelled back.

Edith looked bewildered, and angry, "Your sister?" She had large scratches across her face, that stood out against her pale, wrinkled skin.

"Poppy!" Mallory filled in.

"She's not here!" Edith raised her hands in exasperation, "What on earth do you think you're playing at? I'll have you pay for this!"

"Liar!" Benji's shout caught everyone off guard. They watched, baffled, as he lunged forwards towards Edith.

She paused him easily, a hand outstretched, halting the movement of his limbs so that he collapsed to the grass. Her anger flowed from her in waves, and the pressure on Benji's back steadily increased. Aaron rushed forward, all too aware of the feeling of violation at being paused. He skidded to a stop at Benji's side.

Aaron placed his palms on the ground, sending a furious wave of sound through the soil. Unsuspecting of the assault, Edith was thrown across the lawn, tumbling to a stop in a heap.

"Aaron!" Mallory screamed.

"What?"

"She's an old woman, you can't just do that!"

30 minutes prior - Westgate Train Yard

"What do you mean she's gone?"

Aaron frustratedly punched a train carriage. Vibrations flurried throughout the structure, emitting a low, tremulous reverberation. Mallory stood beside him, worriedly playing with her hair. She did not seem surprised by the existence of the abandoned railway, nor the fact that Aaron had been sneaking off to secretly powerlift trains.

She had, however, made her fury apparent, shocking each of them in turn. She had quickly realised they were training themselves for Chikara fights. She would do anything in her power to stop that happening. She knew from experience the dangers those fights posed.

There was a more pressing problem, however. Aaron and Mallory had arrived too late for Poppy, Benji guiltily explained, as she had vanished half an hour ago.

"She said she was going for a piss!" Mikey argued, "We weren't gonna follow her, were we?"

Tugging at his hair, Aaron muttered to himself, "I'm gonna kill her,"

"Well, at least you'd be talking," Benji interjected brightly.

Aaron raised his eyes skyward in exasperation, allowing Benji to catch sight of the bruises on his neck.

"Aaron, you're injured! What happened?"

"Dr Thackery, the counsellor Poppy had to go see when she was younger," Mallory explained, "He attacked Aaron at our house. I really don't think he's prioritising Poppy's best interests,"

Both Mikey and Benji wore shared expressions of disbelief.

"I can't believe we never realised!" mumbled Aaron, rubbing his eyes anxiously, "We should have known,"

Benji crouched beside him, "None of us could have possibly known," he reasoned, "There is something much bigger at work here,"

"And somehow Poppy and Travis are at the centre of it," Mikey added helpfully.

ESSENCE

Aaron panicked, "I've been such a prick, I should have seen this, how did we not see this?"

"None of us saw this coming," Mallory reassured him, "But you have been a bit of a prick," she added.

"I mean, we could all do something right now," Mikey tugged at his cap, "Like, maybe go help them? What with that conspiracy that Edith might be a killer and all?"

"Edith might be a what now?" Mallory demanded. A small moan of despair emerged from Aaron.

Benji cupped his hands around Aaron's face, pulling him forward so their heads touched. He felt Aaron's anger and fear at being violated by Thackery, but also the overwhelming that he felt about Poppy and how he had treated her.

"We'll find her," he promised, "Together,"

"Right losers," Mallory interrupted their moment, "What's the plan then?"

"There isn't one," Aaron groaned pessimistically.

Mallory eyed one of the trains, a thought flowering in her mind, "So together you three can move one of these trains?"

The boys exchanged glances, "Yes,"

Minutes later, the four of them were aboard an abandoned train. It complained as Aaron shunted it forwards using powerful vibrations, aided by Mikey who guided blustering air currents into its back, pushing it from behind. Benji supported them both, using his own ability to increase the power of theirs. Low rumbles of thunder were lost amongst the complaints of the carriage wheels against the tracks.

Mallory's plan was simple. Use the train to get into the Morris estate and then use it as a quick getaway. She was uncertain of the route, but sure she would be able to figure it out. It would just be a matter of following the train tracks.

But Mallory's fatal flaw raised its ugly head.

She had forgotten about the seven-foot-high brick wall at the end of the tracks.

ESSENCE

CHAPTER 8
13:01 The Morris Estate

Edith screeched from beneath Arabella's assault. Her control was broken and Thackery cursed as chaos descended. Travis felt Poppy pull him onto unbalanced feet. She gripped his hand tightly, and he felt an overwhelming sense of safety encompass him. He later learned this feeling was due to Poppy desperately fighting Thackery's attempts to control Travis.

"Give me back my sister!" Arabella was shrieking, a whirling, ghostly banshee. She shouted at Edith, "You took everything away from me,"

It was quickly established in Thackery's mind that it would be very difficult to regain control of the situation. He had lost his leverage against Poppy, and he could see that Joseph had been triggered. Even he recognised the early signs of an oncoming PTSD attack. He cut his losses and darted out of the room, only to remember he had left the confession there when he was halfway down the drive.

Edith finally managed to separate herself from her crazed granddaughter, scarpering from the room as well in a bid to escape. As she flung herself into the kitchen, she caught sight of the devastation the crashed train had done to her carefully manicured garden. She howled in rage and erupted like a hurricane.

"What have you done to my garden?!"

Meanwhile, desperate attempts were being made to calm Joseph, but they all proved fruitless. Arabella only just managed to dive out of the way as Joseph, in a bid to escape the confinement of the house, barrelled from the parlour into the kitchen.

Joseph threw himself through the backdoor, stumbling across the garden. The noise of the crash had triggered something. A vital component had slipped and failed in his mind, and his supressed memories careened around, loose and ungraspable.

He managed several faltering steps before he collapsed to his knees, struggling to gather his erratic thoughts. He sensed rather than felt the flames. A brightness surrounded him, flashing explosions piercing his eyelids.

Poppy flinched as thunder crashed overhead. Flames encircled Joseph's prone figure in the centre of the garden. The wind whipped the flames into miniature spiralling cyclones. It was a scene of biblical proportions as the first fork of lightning lit up the sky.

She still held onto Travis' hand, despite the fact that Thackery had now disappeared.

Suddenly her siblings were rushing across the grass towards her, spraying up clumps of mud. Aaron reached her first, crushing her in an embrace. Mallory reached them seconds later, hugging them both.

"Oh thank God you are okay," Aaron grinned, pulling away. His eyes widened as an important thought occurred to him, "Did either of you get my message?" he demanded, "About the fact that your therapist is a psycho?"

"Phone's dead," Travis sheepishly admitted.

"I lost mine," Poppy confessed, "But I do know that now, yes,"

"Where is he?" Mallory questioned, furious about Thackery's mistreatment of her sister and his attack on her brother.

"I don't know, he's gone. He ran out the front door," Before Poppy had finished, Mallory had already sprinted into the house to find Thackery.

"I'm sorry Poppy," Aaron hugged her again, "I was just-"

"Apologise to her later, we need to help him," Travis said quickly, indicating Joseph, "I need to get to him, so I can calm him down otherwise he's going to do some serious damage,"

"Pleased to see you alive, Lee," Aaron smacked him spiritedly on his shoulder, "I'm sure we can manage that,"

Aaron left them to retrieve Mikey and Benji, and Poppy turned to Travis, "I can help you," she insisted, "I can calm him, like I did with Margaret. I'm not like Thackery, I promise I won't hurt him,"

He held her face in his hands and kissed her gently on the forehead, "Hey, I trust you, okay?"

"Okay,"

"I couldn't do this without you,"

However, Poppy began to have second thoughts when they reached the edge of the flames. They reached upwards, licking towards the clouds. Another bolt of lightning skewered the heavens and it only seemed to make the fire angrier. It burned her cheeks; she was sure she could feel her eyebrows sizzling.

"I don't think we can get through that," she said doubtfully. Travis' expression reflected her sentiment.

"Yes, you can," Aaron appeared suddenly beside them, flanked by Mikey and Benji. The past hour had taken its toll on the three of them, and they all looked wild and unkempt.

"We can create a bubble, you just focus on calming him down," Aaron directed.

Aaron laid out the plan. Benji nodded in agreement, trusting Aaron completely. Mikey only agreed because it meant playing with fire. Placing a hand on each of Aaron and Mikey's shoulders, Benji slipped easily into his role of support.

Aaron focused on the vibrating air particles that carried the heat across the garden. He gently took control, accomplishing the opposite of what he usually did, and calmed the particles. This cooled a bubble of air, allowing Poppy and Travis to pass through without being burned.

Mikey utilised the growing winds of the storm, directing the air currents into the flames. He tugged the fire apart like a curtain, creating a path to Joseph. Poppy squeezed Travis' hand, and he returned the gesture. Together they walked towards Joseph amongst the flames.

Arabella watched as her cousin and her new friend both bravely entered the inferno to save her great uncle. Her grandmother and the stranger had vanished, perhaps her attack had scared them into retreat.

Or perhaps they were looking for what she currently held in her hands.

The confession was beginning to curl in the heat. Joseph's scrawl at the bottom was almost illegible, but it was there. Arabella thoughts returned to her sister, like they always did when she was about to commit to a rebellious act. Bee missed Bella. The void she left had never been filled. The wound was never allowed to heal, not with Edith's cruel act of displaying Bella's face in the hallway. Bee felt the familiar surge of anger at her Grandmother.

A particularly loud strike of lightning, one that must have struck the earth close by, fuelled her fury.

She growled as she leaned forwards, holding the paper in the flames, and watched it burn.

Joseph was lost.

Lost amongst the tremendous maze of his mind, he was assaulted by visions from his past: vast landscapes torn asunder by the battlefield; the faces of countless soldiers he was unable to save. But then the faces of Anna and Margaret, of Travis filtered in. Battered and betrayed. He had abandoned them all, like he had abandoned those soldiers. He would not be able to save them either. From Thackery and Edith. Or from himself.

"Joseph!" the soldiers were calling his name accusingly. He could sense the venom in their voices. The sounds of their boots marching. The firing of their weapons. He kept his eyes squeezed shut, unable to bear looking upon them. He tried to send them away by haphazardly pushing flames in their direction, but the voices kept calling.

"Joseph, it's me Travis!" His nephew had joined the assault. Couldn't they see how sorry he was?

"I know it seems real Uncle Jay, but it's not. You're here with us, with me and Poppy, okay? We're outside, in the garden," Joseph sensed no anger in Travis' voice. But he wasn't sure he believed him; he could still hear the thunderous sounds of war.

There was a second voice now, gentler, "Joseph, I'm Poppy. We're going to help you. You are in a garden, sitting on the lawn. You can feel the grass, can't you?"

She was right, he could. There were blades of grass between his fingertips, albeit dried from the

heat radiating from him. They rustled whenever he moved. The sounds of battle dulled about him, even the explosions over his head became muffled.

"Can you remember those breathing exercises Mum taught you?" Travis continued, his voice clearer now, "In for 4, out for 7. We'll do it with you,"

A vague recollection occurred to Joseph, of sitting with Anna outside, breathing regularly. He remembered that it had worked last time. This gave him hope. He followed their counting as best as he could.

"Can you take my hand?" Poppy asked softly, "That's it, it feels better, doesn't it?"

Again, she was right. He felt the tension in his limbs begin to ebb. The rapid, painful beating of his heart slowed, the tightness in his chest loosened. The breathing exercises became easier, and the sounds of his memories began to fade.

Poppy and Travis helped him to his feet and slowly guided him out of the flames.

Mallory slid to a halt in the doorway of the parlour. It had been ransacked. Cushions had been flung carelessly, tables overturned, fragile china teacups smashed. Ashes had even been pulled from the fireplace. She continued forwards, out into the front garden, to find Thackery hurtling along the driveway. He was too far away for her to catch him now!

"Hey!" she screamed hopelessly, beginning to sprint after him anyway, "Thackery!"

He glanced over his shoulder, saw her chasing him and skidded to a halt, spraying gravel into the air. He raised his hands and, although still far away, was able to slow the movement of her limbs. Despite her resistance, Mallory found herself slowing. She felt like she was in a dream, her body moving sluggishly. She yelled in frustration as she watched Thackery turn and begin to run again. She could not let him get away, not after everything he had done!

But then she felt a familiar tingling at the base of her scalp. Mallory revelled in thunderstorms. She loved the amount of electricity that hovered between the air particles, the irrevocable sense of potential. She had only ever guided lightning once before; it had resulted in several trees being ignited. She had been told it was an illegal stunt. But at this point, being set aflame was too good a fate for Thackery.

She stopped running. Thackery sensed it and paused again, confused by her sudden inaction. The prickling sensation grew, and all the hairs on her arms stood to attention. Planting her feet firmly, she reached skywards, guiding the flow of electrons to her fingertips.

As the bolt struck, she felt a rush of mind-numbing energy. It was better than any high Imps had given her. It pulsed through every vein, every cell of her body as she redirected it towards Thackery. On release, it burst from her fingers with a deafening bang, crackling and buzzing.

It was over in seconds. Thackery didn't know what hit him. All he saw was a blinding light and suddenly he was lying down. Gravel dug threw his coat. His back hurt.

Mallory sighed, coming down from her high. She marched over to Thackery, some remnants of electricity still crackled in her blood. A burn stretched across his face and neck, a blossoming intricate web where the lightning had passed through his body.

"If you ever come near my family, ever again, I will kill you,"

CHAPTER 9
14:00 – The Morris Residence

Robert waved the fire truck into the back garden. The wheels churned the grass and flowerbeds to mud as it awkwardly manoeuvred around the house. He began barking orders at his team but paused to look at the sky as the first, fat raindrops finally began to fall.

He looked over to the circle of fire, which thankfully seemed to be diminishing now that the source had been calmed and removed. He was glad of the rain. It would help put the flames out.

Anna brought a tray of full, steaming teacups into the living room. The teenagers were sprawled across the uncomfortable sofas, wrapped in blankets. Anna had arrived on the scene to find her son, that girl, and her uncle all in the centre of a fiery inferno. From the immense amount of smoke coalescing with the thunderous clouds in the sky, and the raging sound of the flames crackling, it only took her seconds to realise that her Uncle was suffering from an intense PTSD attack.

She effortlessly created a sound barrier around them, in

an attempt to reduce the crashes of thunder overhead. It helped, as minutes later the flames began to die and Joseph emerged exhausted, propped between Travis and Poppy.

Joseph was now asleep upstairs, weakened from the events of the day. They had put him in Margaret's bed who was thrilled to have been of use. Edith had converted Joseph's old room to a walk-in wardrobe, much to the chagrin of her two daughters at the time. He had slept fitfully amongst dresses and coats, before being transferred at Margaret's insistence. He now seemed content to have a bed to rest in.

As a result, Margaret floated about the house, confusing the policeman with her disconnected stories of her mother. She made several attempts to make tea for everyone, but Anna took over from her when she ripped open all the teabags and poured the loose tea into mugs. She now sat with her daughter, loosely plaiting her hair.

Arabella did not mention the confession. She decided it was her secret to keep. Her own act of rebellion in memory of her sister. When everyone had left, she planned to destroy the cabinet with her sister's mask in. She had collected several bricks from the destroyed garden wall already.

Patrick and Claire Dunkeany stood in the hallway, discussing worriedly the impact Thackery may have had on their children, especially Poppy, with a psychologist brought in with the police. Patrick wore an expression of grim determination, thoroughly prepared to hunt Thackery down himself. Claire struggled to maintain her composure, unable to comprehend how Thackery had managed to get so far on so many lies.

As Anna handed out the mugs of sweet tea, the Detective Inspector was introduced to the room.

"I am DI Anthony Morales, I want to ask you all some brief questions," he announced, "It's important we get clear statement of what occurred today because these events may impact several other cases,"

"What cases?" Poppy asked. She sat beneath a blanket

with Travis, but she had left some space between them. She still feared her own power, worried that is she touched him she might unintentionally hurt him.

"One of those cases will be mine," Anna supplied when the DI refused to answer, "When Joseph returned with some additional evidence, I initiated court proceedings against the company my father sold his business to, claiming that the contract was fraudulent. We're also looking into slander against Jay,"

"The other case will be Daddy's death," Margaret added, undoing the plait she had just finished and beginning again.

"Do any of you know where Dr Thackery and Edith might be?"

"Well, the last I saw of Edith was in the garden, screaming at us," Mallory answered for the six of them.

"And Thackery?"

Only Poppy caught Mallory's brief, satisfied expression before it morphed into one of bewilderment, "I don't know," she said, innocently.

"There is evidence that Thackery was struck by lightning on the front driveway,"

"How unfortunate," Mallory deadpanned, despite the look of disbelief from her siblings. Law-abiding, perfectly behaved Mallory, who never let her temper get the better of her in public? Who always demanded good manners from her siblings? Who refused to take part in even mere discussions of Chikara fights? Could it be possible for that Mallory to have struck Thackery with lightning?

"If it is discovered that it was purposeful, there are very serious charges associated with that," Morales warned.

Mallory met Morales' steely gaze with an equally fierce one, "My abilities are electromotive," she admitted firmly, "But they are weak, I can't handle more than a few hundred volts at any one time, never mind a lightning strike,"

"Will your GP records reflect that?"

Mallory nodded stiffly. She was in full confidence that

they would. Underfunded GP surgeries meant outdated electromotive measuring machines and inaccurate results.

"Which one of you is Poppy Dunkeany? Ah, you, we need to take some details of you so we can get you registered on the Organic Kinaesthetic Registry,"

"What's that?" Travis demanded defensively.

"It's important we keep track of those with this ability," DI Morales explained tactlessly, "Especially after the war. Damage can be done, people can be hurt,"

Thackery's words returned to Poppy, how with this ability she was no closer to being accepted by the population. Yet when she looked about the room, she saw that her friends and family shared the same expression of faint incredulity.

Mikey broke the silence, snorting with laughter, "Poppy saves spiders, and she rehomes the caterpillars she finds in the garden, she's not gonna hurt anyone,"

She was relieved to see everyone nod in agreement. She did not pull away when Travis took her hand, taking courage from the fact that no one believed she would intentionally harm anyone.

"It's the law," DI Morales responded sternly.

The DI eventually left after several more questions. He promised he would back, a vow no one was particularly thrilled to hear. A calmness settled over the room, and several of them slipped into a snooze, exhausted from the events of the day.

Benji dozed, unconsciously resting against Aaron's chest. Splayed uncomfortably in an armchair, Mikey twitched in his sleep. Poppy watched in fascination, "Even in his sleep he doesn't keep still," she muttered to Travis, but he didn't hear her because he had started snoring too.

"Hey Poppy?" Mallory surreptitiously tapped her sister on the shoulder.

"Mm?"

"I think Aaron and Benji might be a thing,"

Poppy recalled the two nights a week that Aaron

disappeared, still unaccounted for, "Yeah I think so,"

"And he never told us,"

"Nope,"

"The little sod,"

"Right?"

"He's done that so I can't take the piss hasn't he?"

"You always promised if he bought someone home that you would immediately get his baby photos out,"

Mallory sighed, shifting into a more comfortable position. Poppy anxiously bit her lip before plunging in and asking, "Did you really strike Thackery with lightening, Mal?"

Mallory glanced around the room through half-lidded eyes, it was empty except for the two of them and the snoozing boys, "Yes," she whispered.

"How? How are you so powerful?"

"There's a few reasons I think, I haven't figured it out yet,"

"You can tell me,"

"Not right now,"

"Why did you do it?"

She glanced up in surprise, "Because he was a monster. He attacked Aaron at home, did you know that? And then there's his abuse of you for God knows how many years,"

"I had accepted that my powerless wasn't a bad thing you know," Poppy said quietly, "But know I'm all confused again,"

Mallory pulled her sister into a hug, "You're smart Poppy, if anyone can figure it out it's you,"

CHAPTER 10
25th December 2019 - The Dunkeany Residence

Christmas arrived, as always, unexpectedly quickly. Despite weeks of preparation, the Dunkeany's found themselves overwhelmed by the season. Christmas cards were sent out late, presents bought last minute (or in Aaron's case, not at all) and Patrick only just managed to get the last Turkey from the butchers.

In the spirit of the season, Claire had agreed to host Travis' family, Mikey and his grandmother, as well as Benji. It had seemed, at the time, a generous and thoughtful proposition. She quickly grew to regret it. During hectic preparations to serve, Claire had muttered something about 'feeding the five thousand' to which Aaron had reasonably responded that there was only fourteen of them and that really wasn't very close to five thousand at all and did she want help pulling that turkey from the oven because it looked like she had got it stuck?

Claire's retort was to throw a homegrown carrot at her son's head.

Later, when everyone had entered the food coma phase, Joseph quietly took Poppy aside.

"I have met several Organic Kinaesthetics in my time," he began bluntly, "Many of them abused their powers like Thackery,"

Poppy did not respond, conscious that Joseph was about to say something important.

"I feared for my nephew," he admitted gruffly, "I told him you were dangerous. But I was wrong, and I want to apologise for that. I admire the strength you showed in that room,"

"Thank you,"

The conversation left her feeling hopeful. She had decided she still wanted to work with those children who failed to develop an ability, as well as those who struggled to control it. She chose her A-levels to reflect this, determined to use her newfound powers to make a difference in the world.

However, each month, she was to physically attend her own therapy sessions. This doubled as a record of her whereabouts to be documented on the Organic Kinaesthetic registry.

She still believed, despite the changes over the past few months, that she belonged here, with her family and friends. That she could be accepted and loved for who she was.

Several months later, Travis and Poppy visited the zoo. Together, they walked to the elephant enclosure, leaning over the railings like they had all those years ago. The old elephant remembered, despite the intervening years.

It moved hurriedly indoors as soon as it saw them, unwilling to be subjected to the weird sensation of having its colour changed again.

"Aw, there goes the last elephant," Poppy waved sadly as its swinging behind disappeared inside.

"I don't think they like it anyway," Travis laughed. He had tried practicing on the neighbour's cat, but now it hissed and scarpered whenever it saw him. He resolved to leave animals alone.

They meandered away from the enclosure, admiring the other animals that sunned themselves in the bright spring sunlight.

"There are so many things I am glad about," Poppy announced suddenly.

"Like what?"

"That Joseph has finally been cleared, and that he and your aunt are getting the help they need and that we became friends again,"

Travis smiled, once again in awe of Poppy. She was beautiful in the sunlight, and he still could not believe she wanted to spend all her time with him.

"Yeah," he agreed, "I'm glad too,"

ESSENCE

MORE BY THIS AUTHOR

The Devil Calls

Melanie Parker celebrates her 18th birthday on the day of her best friend's funeral. She struggles to take the ceremony seriously as it utterly fails to represent Cass truthfully. But it is an ending, a big, black full stop to Cass, a reminder that she is never coming back. That is until Cowan tells Mel he's been seeing her ghost.

The truth behind her death is soon uncovered and Mel and Cowan must work to prevent Cass's fate from happening to anyone else. But it's all too soon before they are trapped too, being led down the same overgrown, rarely walked path as the others.

They are unable to ignore the irresistible beckoning in their desperation to find the truth. The Devil Calls and they are powerless to ignore it.

Gormless

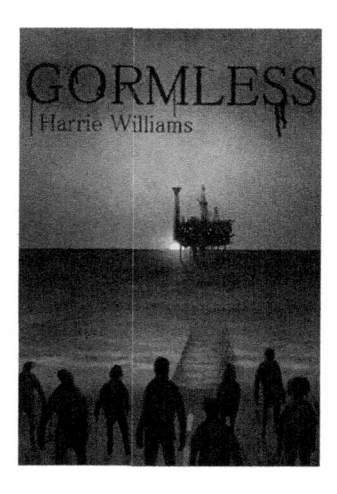

"Everyone had already decided what I was and who I was. I realised I had simply accepted it."

The world descended into chaos when the man-made infection broke out. Eight years later, survivors exist in an apocalyptic world, ruled by the mindless Gormless. Kitt has spent most of her life at the Sanctuary, following the rules of dreary existence based on primal survival. But then there is the possibility of Immunity. Of a cure. Of a life without fear. As her already uncertain world enters the world of volatile unpredictability, Kitt attempts to keep her family safe from the Gormless and the imminent thread from the city. She just has to stay in control.

Moments

"We do not remember days, we remember moments." - Cesare Pavese. This collection of poems aims to capture the small, enjoyable, seemingly insignificant moments that build the fabric of our memories and find the beauty in the most simplistic aspects of our natures.

Printed in Great Britain
by Amazon